SIRENS

Life in Rural Germany During and Shortly after World War II

Ursula (Winter) Turner

Sirens

For Information:
Ursula Turner
uturnj@sbcglobal.net

Copyright © 2008 Ursula Turner
Author Edited
Cover: Richard Henry

ISBN   978-0-9788520-8-7

Library Congress Control Number   2007942190

1. Historical novel - World War II - Germany
2. Allendorf - Launsbach
3. Winter family
4. Historical fact - bombings

All rights reserved. No part of this book may be reproduced or transmitted in any form or by any means electronic or mechanical, including photo copying, recording, or by any information storage and retrieval system without written permission from the copyright owner.

Tanos Books publishing

1110 West 5th Street
Coffeyville, Kansas, 67337
www.tanosbookspublishing.com

Printed in the United States of America

Ursula (Winter) Turner

Foreword

Born in Germany during World War II, the music of Ursula (Winter) Turner's early childhood was not happy melodies. Instead, her days were filled with air raid sirens, the drone of planes, and then the explosions.

Ursula writes, *"Although I could sense the fear in the adults, all this was nothing unusual for me. It was a regular occurrence. I wasn't use to any other kind of life, and I was much too young to understand what the others were afraid of."*

"Sirens: Life in Rural Germany during and Shortly after World War II," is a vivid first-hand account of war through a child's eyes. Americans are used to viewing this war through the eyes of the Allies, but here Ursula shares the flip side. She painstakingly recreates life in Allendorf: the incessant bombings, ill health and hunger, and worry for her father, a prisoner of war. In doing so, she reminds us that war is no respecter of sides; that horrors and heroism, pain and love flourish everywhere during wartime.

Ursula (Winter) Turner's memories and recreations ring with an authenticity that will always elude filmmakers. She fills her rich story with matter-of-fact detail that illuminates and informs the reader. *"Sirens"* is an important book both for its historical value and its ability to entertain. I heartily recommend it for all those seeking to better understand the way life really was during World War II.

- Chuck Bowman, Hollywood producer, director, actor, and writer.

Sirens

Ursula (Winter) Turner

Dedication

To my children and grandchildren and all those yet to come. May they never have to experience the horrors of a world war.

Karl Winter   *Erna Winter*

Sirens

Acknowledgements

I want to thank all my friends and relatives who lived through the terrors again by helping me remember incidents and events we all experienced during those dark days of World War II

First and foremost I want to thank my sister Mechthild (Winter) Walter who still lives on the second floor of the house our parents built in their hometown, Launsbach.

I also want to thank Elsa (Gotthard) Reifenrath, my childhood friend who still lives in the town of my birth, Allendorf, where we experienced the war years together.

Elisabeth (Würtz) Garrison married an American soldier and is currently making her home near Dallas, Texas.

Although Karin (Tetschlag) Hamilton did not share our war experiences, she lived through her own horrors when the Russians came to Berlin, her birthplace. She now lives in Kansas along with her American husband.

Hannelore Wittenbecher was born and raised in Communist East Germany and still lives there, even though the borders are open and the fence is gone.

Thanks go to my cousins Wolfgang Kümmel and Dieter Uth who provided memories as well as pictures.

To my friend, Lois Hendrix and her photography skills, I thank her for her time for taking my picture.

All these people were instrumental in making this book a reality.

Ursula (Winter) Turner

Introduction

I've tried my best to relate the events in this book as accurately as possible according to recollections of my experiences in World War II. It is reasonable to assume that, due to my young age, I did not ingest the horrors of the war the same way an adult would and also can not possibly remember all that happened. However, there were incidents that left deep impressions on my mind, events that I felt the need to record. I did have help from others, some older than I, who remembered more of the happenings documented in this book. In some cases, because so many of the participants have died, or the memories of those still alive have grown dim, I have taken certain liberties and filled in the blanks the way I thought something might have happened, in order to make some of the stories complete. Consequently some of the incidents in this book may not be one hundred percent accurate, but they will, nevertheless, give the reader a chance to experience the wartime and postwar-time years through the eyes of someone who was there.

Ursula (Winter) Turner

From left, Mechthild, me at 3 months, and Mutti. This was the only studio photo in our possession.

Sirens

Preface

My mother, Erna Winter, faithfully wrote a letter to my father, Karl, every single day while he was serving in World War II. He answered her letters when he could and our mother sent my older sister, Mechthild, and me to the post office every day to see if mail had arrived.

Then, one day in March 1944, 27 of Mutti's letters were returned – Papa was declared missing – and she did not hear from him again until March 1945. However, she was notified in February of '45 that he was a prisoner of war in France, being held by the Americans.

During the long, agonizing wait to hear from him, Mutti decided to write a journal in which she noted everything of importance to her – everything she would normally have put into her daily letters, and wrote her journal in that style, as though she were writing to him directly.

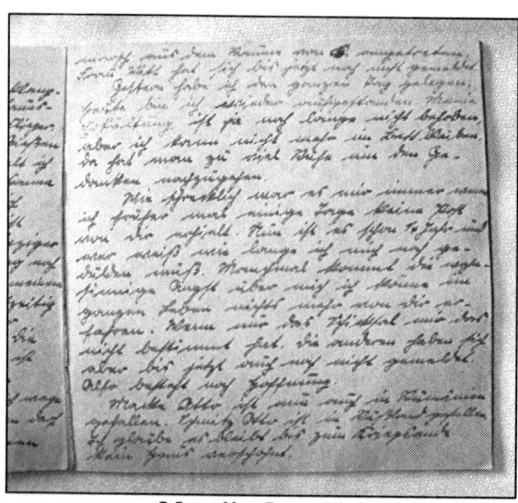

Mutti's Journal

Ursula (Winter) Turner

Mutti's Journal

<u>November 21, 1944</u>
On Thursday, November 16, I received the letter from the Company. I had waited for such a long time, but I don't know any more than I did before. They don't know anything about where you are either. Tomorrow is my birthday and I don't know if you are alive. How happy we were a year ago when I was with you in Aachen[1]. How things have changed since then.

On that Thursday I had taken Mechthild to Launsbach. I had asked Mamma[2] to call me immediately should she hear from you. I've been waiting a quarter of a year already, and on this day the letter from the Company arrived. I was called to the telephone and can't describe the thoughts that went through my head and how my heart pounded when I went to answer the phone. I had slight hopes that there was news from you directly, but I guess I am not that lucky. At least I was able to tell your parents about the letter right away. It is particularly hard for your mother since Heinz[3] has been declared missing in action in Russia for some time now.

Originally we were supposed to stay until Saturday morning, but I could not rest; I wanted to see the letter for myself. We left Friday morning with the 5 o'clock train and should have arrived in Haiger at 7 o'clock. One can only travel in darkness these days because of the low-flying fighter planes. Just last Thursday the 2 o'clock train was shot at near Sechshelden. The attack left three dead, nine critically injured and ten others with lighter injuries. At 7 o'clock

---
[1] A city in Germany
[2] Mutti's mother often stayed with us during the war.
[3] Her grandson

Sirens

we arrived in Dillenburg. There we were told that a speeding passenger train had run into a freight train near the train station in Sechshelden. We all had to exit our train and walk around the accident site. On the other side a train was waiting to take us to Haiger. Everything was so complicated that we did not make it there until 9:30. I already had a cold, and on the train ride it got worse. Nevertheless, I took my bicycle to Niederroßbach the same day. Frau Pfeiffer[4] had received the same letter as mine from the Company. Also 17 letters she had written to her husband had been returned to her with the note: Wait for new address. Until now I have had 27 letters returned, with 45 cigarettes – all mail for which you have been waiting for for half a year now. If only the day arrived... (I had to go into the basement again)[5] when you received news from me and I received news from you. Because I will not believe that you are no longer here.

On the way home from Niederroßbach it started to snow and after that, my cold got really bad. At home I immediately went to bed and just got up a little while ago. However, my cold is not gone yet. But one cannot relax in bed. The bombers take care of that. Off and on I had to get out of bed and run into the basement.

On Sunday it was really bad. All around us the bombs and Bordwaffen (VBW or vertical on-board weapons[6]) crashed. In Rodenbach a bomb fell into the center of town so that 20 homes had to be evacuated. Three people died. The Siegen and Cologne railroad line was hit so that many trains were late again. Just now I hear the growling of a number of planes again, and it is time for Mechthild to be on her way home... (again in

---

[4] Her husband served with Papa
[5] She frequently had to interrupt her journal to seek shelter in the basement from bombers
[6] Author's note

the basement) from school. A person cannot stay calm any more.

Today I received a letter from Frau Lipp[7]. She also received a letter from the Company, but it was different from mine and Frau Pfeiffer's. According to her letter her husband was no longer with your group and did not leave there until August 29, while the rest of you were supposed to have left August 27.

Richard Benner[8] is one of the lucky ones who got out. He has lately been writing a lot about Kolmar. Now Frau Pfeiffer tells me that Frau Benner has received a letter from the maintenance office in Gießen, asking for information about her dead husband in Fellerdilln. We hope this is a mistake. Frau Benner would be a lot worse off than we, should this be true. She had the first difficult weeks just like we did, then the joy when he wrote, and now this misfortune. At least there is still hope for us that you are alive and will write some day. How we have waited for Benner to come home on leave and to hear details from him. He had counted on getting a three-day-leave. Others had already left. In his first letter he wrote about having an infection in his hand, and in one of his last ones he wrote that it was worse. Perhaps this is why he died. But let us hope it is all a mistake. Should you really not come back, I could not in any way wish that others will have the same misfortune. You will be back. I dream so often about you, and you are always healthy and happy. Just last night I saw you before my eyes. As long as there is no word from the others, there is hope.

November 24, 1944

My birthday has passed without fanfare. Even from Launsbach nobody came because of the bombers. On November 21 they threw bombs on Wetzlar and

---

[7] Her husband served with Papa
[8] He served with Papa

Sirens

Gießen. From Gertrud[9] I received a birthday letter yesterday, from Hanna[10] today. They all wish for me that I will receive news from you soon. That is also my biggest and only wish. When I heard nothing from you by Mechthild's birthday[11] I assumed I would get mail by the time my birthday came around, but I shuddered at the long time I would have to wait. And now that time has passed and still there is nothing. Must I now place my hopes on Christmastime? I almost do not dare. I simply cannot think of Christmas. Almost daily news arrives from prison camps. Soon something should arrive from you. From the five who did not give a sign from the West, only one has written from a prison camp. I wish with all my heart that we will hear from all of them. Of course, my heart is not easy when I think of you as a prisoner of war, but it is better than if I, some day, receive the news of your death.

The thing with Richard Benner was a mistake as Frau Pfeiffer let me know yesterday. Frau Lipp told me that, she too, has received a letter from the Company. Her husband was transferred to 13th Company and has been retreating since August 29. I have not heard from Frau Witt[12].

Yesterday I was down all day. Today got up again. My cold is still not gone, but I can't stay in bed any longer because there I have too much time to think.

How awful it always was in the past when I did not receive mail from you for a few days. Now it has been a quarter of a year, and who knows for how much longer I will have to be patient. Sometimes this horrible fear comes over me that I will not hear from you for the rest of my life. Schmitt's Otto[13] was killed in action in

---

[9] Mutti's sister
[10] Papa's sister
[11] October 13
[12] Her husband served with Papa
[13] A neighbor

Russia. I think that by the time the war is over not one house will be spared.

February 2, 1945
It has been a long time since I wrote. Since I can no longer write to you, dear Karl, I lack the desire to write. Much has happened in the meantime, but mail or any other sign of life from you I still have not received. How much longer will I have to wait? Because I know for certain that you are still alive. Through some circumstances you are simply not able to get any news to me. I have calmed down quite a bit lately, even though the yearning for you is still there.

On Tuesday Heinrich Weber[14] wrote from an American prison camp. He had not written since July, and this was a pre-printed card which was sent October 29. It took a quarter of a year to get here. His wife cannot write him since she does not know his address. At least she knows he is alive. That kind of news would be enough. How I would revive from such news. (Mutti then names ten men who have written from prison camps and who have not written since.[15])

We went to Launsbach for Christmas and New Years. On the third of January my mother butchered a pig, and on the fifth we came back home. We had luck on the train trip. On the way there we had immediate connections and on the way home as well. All those trains ran without a timetable. Because of the bomb attacks in Gießen all trains were detoured along our route. All the trains stopped at every station along the way.

On December 3 there had already been an attack on Gießen, then came a big one on December 6 through which almost the entire city was destroyed, and then there was another bombing on December 16. There is

---

[14] A neighbor
[15] Author's note

Sirens

not much left of Gießen. Also Kleinlinden and Heuchelheim have been hit hard. Officially there were 400 deaths.

    Nothing at all happened in Launsbach during those raids, but we got our share on the afternoon of Christmas Eve. We had just finished eating at my mother's. Mechthild and Ursula were with Winter Oma[16]. Then the sirens started. The bombers had been buzzing above us for a while. Suddenly there was a crash, and another, and another. Everybody headed for the basement, but luckily nothing had happened to any of us or we would not have been able to run to the basement unharmed. I was worried about the children because it was not difficult to guess that bombs had dropped all over the village. But what had they hit? We could not get away because the Flak (Fliegerabwehrkanonen – aircraft defense cannon.[17]) were shooting and in Gießen a solid covering of bombs was still falling. From the window in the stairwell we could see a bomb crater in the Schützenweg, also that the factory had been hit several times. When it quieted down a bit, I started off. I could not go up the Burgweg because it had been closed due to some duds. So I ran through downtown. It looked like a wasteland. Korl's house had collapsed. People were crawling out from under falling chunks of brick. Aside from small injuries they were alright, which was a small miracle. There were nine bomb craters in the yard of Rinn's Tavern. Two bombs fell on Rinn's stable. It had collapsed and buried all the animals under it. Although the clean-up was started immediately, the animals could not be saved. Four cows, two pigs and a goat perished. The factory was hit three times. One was a dud. A bomb fell in front of Henny's house. One big bomb, weighing almost a ton, fell on Stroh's bakery. Luckily it, too, was

---

[16] Papa's mother
[17] Author's note

a dud. One fell in Stroh's garden and another, also a dud, fell in Helga Jermelcher's garden. Two fell into Winter Rudolf's garden. One dud fell on the nursery, one fell next to the Rau's house and one fell next to Stork's, close to our building lot. A number of bombs fell in the fields along the hillside. I guess the first crater was up in the woods and the last ones fell on Korl's house. I think they got hit by three bombs. I counted a total of 38 bombs but was told there might have been as many as 70. The craters are all sizes. You can imagine that there were broken windows as well as roof tiles. There was no electricity or water for a week. Winter Oma had some broken windows and a few roof tiles were broken on the barn. We had two large holes in the barn roof as well as numerous broken roof tiles.[18] The cobble stones from the factory yard flew as far as our yard. Through all this excitement I made it through Christmas Eve. However, New Year's Eve was that much harder to get through.

Since we have come back home, a lot of single bombs have fallen in this area. How often we have sat in the basement, day and night. Just a few days ago there was another big attack on Siegen. The little things I do not even remember much any more. Siegen is pretty much done for, too. Yesterday evening a bomb fell on Holzhausen which we could hear. One immediately jumps off one's chair to grab the things that are ready to be taken to the basement. It really isn't much since we keep a lot of our clothes down there now.

Pfeiffer's Margot came on Monday and stayed until today. She went from here to Haiger to school because the road from Niederroßbach was too difficult because of the snow. Since Wednesday it's been real bad again with the bombers, and on Friday Margot got sick. Because of that, I went to get Frau Pfeiffer and today she took her home with her. Ursula has been

---

[18] At her mother's house

down and in bed since Tuesday with another bad cold. It is not pleasant when the bombers come and there are sick people that have to go to the basement. Mechthild does not want me to stay upstairs. She has been terribly afraid since the bombing attack in Launsbach. She is also afraid to go to school now. Usually she has to walk home since the trains either do not run at all because of air raid alarms, or they are real late. Since we have returned from vacation we have made a bed for Ursula here in the living room. I had been sleeping here on the sofa anyway. Oma[19] and Mechthild sleep in Mechthild's room. Our bedroom remains unused.

February 13, 1945

Today Ernst Hoffmann[20] wrote a letter as a prisoner of war of the French. Now you are the only one here in the village from whom there has not been any word at all. I am glad they have heard from Ernst; that strengthens my hope that you are still alive. And yet I received a blow from this. How light and happy I would feel if I would finally hold a card from you in my hands. Ernst mailed his card on November 12. It was en route for a quarter of a year. He writes that he has been a prisoner of war since August 31. Perhaps he sent a pre-printed card that has not yet arrived.

On Thursday Oma went back to Launsbach. She did not know when she would return. Of course, as soon as she was gone, I got sick. Saturday I had to stay in bed. Half an hour ago I had to get up but only because a bomb threw me out of bed. One does not even get exited about this any more. Only, it is better to be dressed. I do not feel well at all and in a little while I will lie down again. It is not anything more than a cold. In the past something like that could not have gotten me down. Today I lack the spirit. Yes, if I knew you were still

---

[19] Her mother, whom we called Lenchen Oma or just Oma.
[20] A neighbor

alive then everything would be different. Yesterday evening I no longer had a fever, and this morning it is back. The cause is probably that I have not slept all night long. I was thinking of you constantly and painted the worst pictures in my mind. Mechthild will have to miss school, since Oma is not here, and take care of the household. It will not hurt her.

Just now we came back from the basement. Low flying planes have been working Haiger over for about half an hour. This is a daily occurrence. It is a wonder nothing has happened here yet. We have always been sorry that we did not have a train station. Today we are glad that we do not.

I received a letter from Karl Löber[21] today. He has been trying hard to find out something about Jäger from Hofgeismar. He did discover that he does not live in Hofgeismar but in Eberschütz. The letter was dated February 8. In it Karl writes that this Jäger had sent the red card from prison camp at the beginning of January already, in other words, four weeks ago. Why... (back in the basement) a big truck has wrecked at the corner of Weyel's; one upset after another. Why am I not getting any news if you are still alive? My peace of mind is gone again. I am so worried about you. The day after tomorrow it will be half a year since you last wrote. Two from Hofgeismar made it out at the retreat. They supposedly wrote that part of the Company went to prison camp as one group. Who is among the, one almost wants to say, lucky ones? Should you happen to be one of them, I would think I will soon hear something.

Herman Bittendorf[22] has also written from a prison camp. He is in Africa.

Tomorrow it will be two weeks since Oma left for Launsbach and so far I have not even heard if she

---

[21] He taught school along with Papa and lived next door to us
[22] A neighbor

Sirens

arrived there. That is something that cannot be taken for granted these days. If I only heard from you, then everything would be alright.

<u>February 25, 1945</u>
Finally I have news that you are in a prison camp. What that means to me can only be felt by those who have been in the same situation. I am so happy. After all the months of worried waiting I now have a feeling of happiness such as I have never experienced before. How much the sorrow has weighed on me I only discovered after it was taken away. You are sitting behind barbed wire and are probably already hoping for mail from me, and I just now received your card. It will be several months until you receive my first letter. I wrote right away. How glad I am that I am finally able to write to you, and I am looking forward to your first letter. It will probably be a while before it gets here, but I have patience now. I finally know that you are alive. Now everything will be alright again. But now I have to describe this day and how it went.

The night before, we did not get out of our clothes. We were barely asleep when isolated bombs fell again. That is how it went all night long. By morning we had been in the basement five times and that is not a small matter with children, especially the little one who simply would not wake up. The next morning, Sunday, the same thing continued, and now they shoot off Bordwaffen as well. They went back and forth between Herborn and here. We thought at any moment a bomb would fall on our roof. At least we do not have to worry about Bordwaffen when we are in the basement.

When they took a small break, we ran quickly upstairs so I could fix lunch, which I managed, and we were even able to eat in peace. After that I planned to bake some waffles for the afternoon. I barely got started

Ursula (Winter) Turner

when the doorbell rang and Frau Würtz[23] was standing there. She said, "Frau Winter, your husband has written." At first I did not understand what she meant, but then I fell on my knees and thanked God and I laughed and cried at the same time. How much I had begged God during the last six months he may keep you safe. Not one evening did I forget to pray. At first, of course, Mechthild, Ursula and Oma were told the news. Little Ursula said, "Mutti, you don't have to cry if Papa has written. You have to be glad." Then I told the Löbers and Lindmeyers, the Schols, and the Frankfurters. Everybody in the house cried tears of joy. All of them knew how much I had suffered. I did not have your card at this time. It was still in Haiger. They had called Frau Würtz from the post office. Mechthild was to get the card. She immediately got on her bicycle and rode to Haiger. She had barely left when the sirens sounded again. Now she sits in the basement there and we here.

    Now all hell broke loose. Here it was mostly the crashing noise of the Bordwaffen, but in Niederscheld and Herborn they let loose with the bombs. During a break, Mechthild came home with the card. Then it started up again. Only now it was much worse. In the woods stood a freight train at which they shot, but they also dropped bombs on it. This train was loaded with ammunition. Suddenly that exploded into the air. Luckily only one car was hit and courageous railroad employees unhooked this car and moved it away. You could hear the explosions until 2 in the morning. As the bombs dropped and the Bordwaffen crashed, we thought our last hour on earth had come. And just now, after you have written, I want to live a little longer. I do not think I should write you how it is here right now. You would not have a peaceful moment. At 5 a.m. the all-clear finally sounded. So I got on my bicycle and rode to

---

[23] She apparently had a phone or worked where there was one

Niederroßbach. It was hard for Frau Pfeiffer because I now have mail and she does not. But that is life. It could have been the other way around. In the evening I wrote to everybody in Launsbach, to all the wives[24] and finally to you. At 11:30 p.m. I fell into bed, dead tired. That was, despite everything that happened, the happiest day of my life. Only one day can be better, that is the day when we stand facing each other.

Yesterday and today, and during both nights, we had peace. Today all citizens above the age of six were geröntgt (x-rayed). Ursula insisted she wanted to be geräuchert (smoked). I told her that such little girls would not be x-rayed, but she told me, "Mutti, please go with me and tell them Ursula wants to be smoked and then you can leave." And she told Oma, "Oma, you are so old, you can let yourself be smoked." When all the others were done, I let her be x-rayed and she said, "Mutti, that did not hurt at all."

Oma came back Friday. She had to overcome a few hurdles to get here because the train tracks had been bombed on Wednesday and Thursday in several places. The train station in Haiger had been hit severely and the trains only went as far as the bridge over the Dill River. Passengers had to walk from there to the Allendorfer Straße where they were able to board another train and continue their journey. All people had to travel this way, or in reverse, for a while until the tracks were fixed. Also, the road to Dillenburg was blocked because it got hit badly near the train station in Haiger. But all that was soon fixed. The trains were barely back in operation when those things happened on Sunday. Now people have to walk from Haiger to Würgendorf before they can catch a train. I have heard that on Thursday nine bombs were dropped on Haiger. A few houses were hit. But only two people died.

---

[24] Of Papa's fellow soldiers

Ursula (Winter) Turner

<u>March 3, 1945</u>

How often we have been back to the basement again. At night we go to bed fully dressed so that we are always ready. I do not even undress Ursula any more. In the evenings, when we are in the kitchen, we fix her a bed on two chairs so that we will always have her nearby. Only when we go to bed do I put her in hers. Every hour of the night the monsters are here. It is always good when we do not hear them so we do not lose as much sleep. This morning they came already before 9 o'clock. Usually they left us alone until around 10. In Haiger they again dropped a lot of bombs today. Luckily most of them missed their targets. Besides a lot of broken window panes in town, the school was demolished because two bombs fell into the school yard. How will it all end? Even the people in the big cities think that the attacks here are worse than theirs. There they can sit in bunkers, and when the attack is over, it is over. But when the bombers come here, they might come back within five minutes, and there are no safe shelters. We are safe in the basement against shootings, but those planes also carry bombs. When one hears their drone, one must run because a lot can happen in the next moment. The sirens usually do not go off until the bombers are already here.

You are now safe. I just hope we will survive.

Sirens

Chapter 1
A Rough Beginning

    The insistent noise woke me from a deep sleep. I was sick again and Mutti had given me warm milk with honey stirred into it. I hated warm milk, but the honey made my throat hurt less and I was therefore able to sleep better. But now I was wide awake, listening to the wailing of the sirens.
    I started to shiver because I knew what was coming. It had happened too many times before. Every time the sirens started up it was the same thing and, although I wasn't sure what the danger entailed, I was aware that it was something that everybody I knew was afraid of. They called it bombs and had told me that these would come falling from the sky out of planes and if they dropped on us, they could hurt us or even kill us. I didn't want to be hurt. I knew what that meant but had no concept of death at this time.
    Although it was pitch dark outside, I knew Mutti would be rushing into the room in a moment to snatch me out of my bed. I no longer used the crib in her room since I was old enough now to sleep in the regular-size bed that was set up next to my big sister's in what was now our bedroom. Later on, when things got really bad, Mutti and I slept in the living room, she on the couch and I on a makeshift bed, both wearing our clothes while trying to sleep. My sister Mechthild, eleven years older than I, and Lenchen Oma, Mutti's mother who often came to visit, slept in our bedroom during that time.
    As expected, it didn't take long for Mutti to come to the side of my bed. This was happening so often now that it was becoming routine. She grabbed me out of bed and, hurriedly wrapping a blanket around me, carried me down the long corridor to our apartment's

door and down a flight of stairs with Oma, who had been spending this night on the couch for some reason, and Mechthild close on our heels. We crossed the large, square entrance hall to a narrow door to our far right that opened to the basement stairs and was located next to the main door of the building. By this time Mutti was out of breath and shaking. I was skinny for my age, but at three years I was still quite a load for her to have to haul around, and she still had to negotiate the set of narrow concrete steps that led us to a dark, dank place – the building's basement. Although this part of the basement had no windows, the black-out rules still had to be followed and only a 25-watt bulb was allowed.

Several people were already seated on wooden make-shift benches that lined the walls of this central area of the basement. Smaller rooms branched off in different directions and were enclosed by fence-like dividers that reached up to the ceiling. Each family living in the building had been assigned one of these small rooms for their personal use. There was also a communal laundry room and, down a passage and around a corner, close to the outside entrance, the boiler room was located.

We found a place on one of the benches and made ourselves as comfortable as possible. The basement was cold and Mechthild slipped into a cardigan she hadn't taken the time to put on earlier. Mutti, in her hurry, had forgotten hers and wrapped my blanket around the two of us. Oma huddled forward, elbows on knees, staring at the dirty floor. At her own house in Launsbach she would have had only her cellar to sit in along with my aunt, Mutti's sister, Tante Gertrud, and her three little boys. Here she had more people to visit with if she wanted to and the basement at our building was a little more comfortable than her cellar. However, if you are scared, you don't worry about things like comfort all that much.

We sat and waited. People were still entering our shelter, some descending the same stairs we had taken, others entering from the outside. No matter how crowded it got, everybody was welcome to seek shelter in this basement room.

All these people were our neighbors, some from the building itself, others living in houses nearby. They congregated here for the supposed safety the room provided from the bombs they expected to drop from the sky at any moment. Later my sister scoffed at the idea of this being a shelter. "If the bombs had dropped," she said, "we would have had the entire building on top of us."

In Germany almost all houses and apartment buildings have been and still are being built with cellars or basements. For this reason air-raid precautions during World War II were quickly organized by the authorities.

Houses in small towns usually feature cellars, while city dwellings are more likely to contain basements. Our neighbors came to our basement because it was more comfortable for a lengthy stay than their cellars, where they stored potatoes and turnips, would have been.

In order to turn a basement into an air-raid shelter it was necessary to make sure they were prepared in such a way as to accommodate all the residents of a building, although in small towns such as ours these rules weren't always strictly adhered to. Once inside, the occupants had to be protected from any incident other than a direct hit which would have had, as my sister had pointed out, deadly consequences. Another rule was that a means of escape in case of a "real" emergency (what could be more real than an air-raid?) was available, which would have been impossible for the homeowner to guarantee.

However, the inadequacies of the cellars and basements eventually became apparent in the so-called firestorms during the incendiary attacks on the larger German inner cities, especially Hamburg and Dresden. When burning buildings and apartment blocks collapsed in the raging winds that could reach well over 800 degrees Celsius (1492 degrees Fahrenheit), occupants often became trapped in their basement shelters which had become overcrowded after the arrival of people from other buildings that had been bombed during earlier air-raids. Between 60 and 80 percent of those who died perished from heatstroke or carbon monoxide poisoning rather than the fire itself. Thankfully we never had to worry about that happening to us.

But we did have to worry about regular bombing attacks and now, in our shelter, everybody sat very still, fearfully awaiting his or her fate. Nobody said anything, although an occasional soft moan could be heard.

Soon the drone of planes overhead broke the silence. I watched the adults as they cast their eyes toward the ceiling while their heads turned, following the sound of the approaching planes, seemingly able to see the bombers through the roof of the building as they flew across the sky above the village.

Although I could sense the fear in the adults, all this was nothing unusual for me. It was a regular occurrence. I wasn't used to any other kind of life. And I was much too young to understand what the others were afraid of.

My birthplace. The three open windows at the left are part of our apartment. Left, the bedroom; center, the living room; and at right, the dining room

The Village of Allendorf 1937

I had the misfortune of having been born on a cold and snowy January day in my parents' bedroom, during a horrid time in history, with only a midwife there to help with the birth, and with my father noticeably absent. My birth took place roughly two years after a madman, not even German-born, but head of the German government, had declared war on a big part of the world, and my father had been forced to become one of his soldiers. Having been a teacher before he was drafted into the fighting, he had lived with Mutti and Mechthild in an apartment located on the second floor of the school building. It was customary in the Germany of that time to have the teachers live above the classrooms. But Papa was not teaching right now. He had left to fight in the war, and I knew him only from pictures.

And now this group of women, children and old men, ordinary citizens most of whom had no idea why this war was being fought, sat in the school's basement, waiting for the all-clear to sound, hoping to escape the bombs one more time and return to their homes to go on with their interrupted life.

The Winter family in 1941

Sirens

So far we'd been fortunate. Allendorf was only a small town and there was nothing here that would harm our enemy's war efforts, but one never knew. In any case, we had not been targeted as yet. The small town where my grandparents lived, 50 kilometers (about 31 miles) away had been hit several times – by mistake.

Only about three years old at this time I had learned quickly that the shrill noise that so often roused me from sleep was caused by the air-raid sirens warning us to take cover from approaching bombers. There was actually a pre-alarm, an alarm, and then a warning to let us know there was no more time to waste to seek shelter. During this time, and later as well, I spent a great deal of time in bed, ill with one ailment or another, usually a cold or tonsillitis. The children of World War II Germany were not strong or healthy, mostly due to lack of nutritious food.

Now, once again sitting on a bench in the cold basement, I cuddled up against Mutti under the blanket. My thumb went into my mouth automatically. It was so comforting.

As I looked around the large room I saw many of the same faces that came to this place with each alarm being sounded. Most sat hunched forward on the hard benches, their faces lined with worry and fear. Many held mementos, mostly pictures of loved ones – husbands or sons – fighting in this war. Others clenched their hands around bags they held in their lap, most likely containing valuables such as jewelry or keepsakes they had inherited from their parents or grandparents and wanted to save at all cost. Their homes might be bombed and destroyed this time around, so they took no chances. They wanted to save what they could.

By the time the last sounds of the final warning siren had faded away, the room was crowded with people. The benches had filled quickly and children were sitting on the floor on blankets, at their mothers' feet. Mutti would not allow me to sit on the cold floor because I was sick. She preferred to hold me on her lap and offered my seat to a skinny, short woman by the name of Ruth, who lived across the street. Actually, none of the people in the room were fat. Lack of food and hard work prevented that.

Of course I was not aware of all these details at the time. I learned about all that much later. I only knew that we were in the basement because people in planes with bombs were trying to hurt us and we were supposed to be safe here.

I knew several of the people in the room. My friend Elsa was sitting on the floor near her mother and grandparents. Her father, a farmer, had gone to war like all men of an age to be able to fight. They lived across the street from the school building. Frau Schol, who lived upstairs on the third floor, was there with her two children. Her husband was a soldier as well. She never saw him again. He didn't return from the fighting. Her daughter, Rosel, was my age. Scarlet fever had left her deaf when she was a one-and-a half-year-old, toddler, but that did not stop us from playing with each other. Other people who occupied the benches I recognized as close neighbors whose basements or cellars were not suitable to be used for shelters. Only one face was missing. Detche's Hilde. Although she just had a root cellar in which to seek shelter, she didn't mingle much with her neighbors, even in times of war. She was a recluse and was considered an oddball by the community. Later on hers would be one of the few houses in Allendorf to be hit by a bomb. Hilde was found alive and unhurt among her turnips and sugar beets.

All the faces of the people in the basement looked care-worn and gray. Nobody smiled, even in greeting. As far as they were concerned there was nothing to smile about.

Sirens

Some incidents that took place in that basement left a lasting impression in my young mind and I can still picture them as though they occurred yesterday. This was the case with the Löber family. Herr Löber was a teacher, like my dad and had gone to war just like Papa. And there was Frau Löber, her three children and Löber Oma, Löber being her last name and Oma meaning granny. They lived in the apartment next to ours, the only two on our floor. I remember Löber Oma best from the way she always behaved once she entered the basement during a raid. She was quite short, about 4 feet, 9 inches, and always wore ankle-length, dark-colored skirts or dresses and sensible, old-lady shoes. Her gray hair was braided and twisted into a bun high up at the back of her head. She was a dear old lady, but got frightened to the point of insanity by the bombers. As soon as she reached the basement during the air-raids which she did racing down the stairs as fast as she could manage at her age, she scrambled frantically under one of the benches for what she conceived as added protection from the bombs, and remained there until the all-clear had been given. "Löber Oma was usually a very normal-acting, sensible woman," Mutti told me later on, "but the air-raid sirens scared her senseless, and for some reason she felt better protected with a bench above her."

Afterward, when the all-clear had sounded and the two Luftschutzwärte (air-raid wardens) who were usually stationed at the outside doors to the basement, informed the basement's occupants it was safe to go back to their homes, Löber Oma always needed help to get out from under her special shelter. In spite of her absurd behavior, nobody ever made fun of her.

Sometimes, when the wait for the all-clear seemed interminable and the tension in the room rose with each passing minute, a few of the people waiting out the raid in the school's basement would try to ease their anxiety by finally speaking up, with some of them making an attempt to defend what was going on outside.

"Our economy was in financial ruin," an older woman said in a low voice, as if speaking to herself, "and nobody knew what to do. "Yes," agreed a much younger one who was holding a baby in her arms, an indication that her husband had been home on leave not too long ago. "We needed somebody like Hitler to come along. And when he became our Führer in 1933, he did something about the situation. We had a much better life after that. He truly was our savior."

"But did he have to start this awful war?" wailed a woman who was sitting in a dark corner where she could barely be seen. "Couldn't Hitler have saved us some other way? Just look at how many people are dying?"

Everybody is smiling in this photo. From left: Lenchen Oma, Mutti holding me, Tante Dorle, and Mechthild in front of Papa.

Sirens

I didn't know who this Hitler was then. I just kept hearing his name over and over. Not until much later did I understand what those women had been talking about.

Toward the end of the war Allendorf did get hit by several bombs. Some were aimed at the farm women and children in the fields who were also shot at by low-flying, strafing planes. There was no shelter available to them except the furrows or ditches which were not much by way of protection from the danger coming from above. Some of these people were hit. The outhouses at the bottom of the schoolyard where also shot at and hit for unexplained reasons. School was not in session at this time. In fact, the school in Allendorf held no classes for the last year of the war. German soldiers who had been wounded found temporary shelter in the classrooms until they could be shipped home.

The railroad tracks a half a kilometer (about a third of a mile) from town were bombed repeatedly to stop supply trains. The trains themselves were also targeted a few times. The school building stood at the edge of town on that side, but no bomb was ever, even accidentally, dropped on it.

Sometimes the townspeople took advantage when trains were bombed since they often carried goods that were useful and they frequently remained at the bomb site for a while until the area could be cleaned up and the train cars removed. On one occasion word spread that a train had been attacked that held huge rolls of something similar to wax paper. Mutti got out the wheelbarrow and the three of us headed toward the train wreckage. It was a good thing the road went uphill on the way there when the wheelbarrow was empty. The rolls of paper where extremely heavy and Mutti and Mechthild had to struggle to get one loaded into the wheelbarrow. I, of course, was of no help. And then Mutti sprained her ankle. The train had been bombed while in the woods and she tripped over a root.

But we got the roll of paper home and Mutti used it for years, mostly to wrap sandwiches and to make sewing patterns. There is still a bit of it left today, more than 60 years later.

Mutti never attempted to get anything else from a bombed train, however. That sort of action wasn't in her nature, even if it was sometimes necessary for survival during the war.

Sirens

Chapter 2
Everyday Life during the War

During my childhood years I was always sickly. I can still see myself, lying either in my bed or on the living room couch feeling hot and cold in turn and suffering from a sore throat. I spent many days – and nights – on that couch, especially if I happened to be sick during the coldest days of winter. Wood was scarce, coal even more so. Consequently the bedrooms were rarely heated. The living room was always kept warm unless the pile of wood was dangerously low, since our lives were lived in that room. We even ate there in winter while we had our meals in the kitchen during the warmer months.

With each new bout with tonsillitis or whatever else ailed me at any given time during the winter, I was moved to the living room couch, bedding and all. Each time I found it difficult to fall asleep because the mantle clock chimed on the hour and half hour. For the first few days this was impossible to ignore, but eventually I got used to the noise and soon did not hear it at all.

If I spent my sick days in my own bed, Mutti came in every morning to air out the room. Our windows opened inward, one half to each side, and she flung these wings open as far as they would go no matter what the temperature was outside. Then she came over to my bed and tucked the covers around me until only my head stuck out. "Be sure to stay under the covers," she invariably said, then left the room to tend to other things. After about ten minutes she returned to close the window. I did enjoy the fresh air that filled my room while the window had been open. I generally slept on Mechthild's side of the bed when she wasn't there because it was closer to the window and door.

While Mutti always strove to make me feel better, one of her cures, as far as I was concerned, bordered on torture. In retrospect, I'm sure it was a good method of making my sore throat feel better in lieu of more modern practices. She boiled a number of potatoes in their skin, letting them cool enough when they were done not to burn me. She then stuffed them into one of my long, woolen winter stockings, leaving the toes and top empty so she could place this primitive heating pad around my neck while tying the ends in the back. The potatoes held their soothing warmth for a long time and did make my throat feel better, but I was very uncomfortable as I lay in my bed and I had to stay on my back because it was difficult to turn on my side with the potatoes wedged under my neck. When the potatoes were cold, Mutti would take them out of the stocking and peel them and then either fry them or make potato salad. Nothing was ever wasted.

I was often bored when I had to spend a lot of time in my bedroom although I did sleep a lot if I had a fever. During the war years I was not yet old enough to have learned how to read. Television was unheard of, and the radio was kept in the living room. There wasn't much aired anyway besides propaganda for the war and the Vaterland, whatever that meant. I had heard this man named Hitler whom the women in the basement had mentioned, talk on the radio on several occasions. Mutti said he was the Führer. I didn't like to listen to him because he screamed so much.

So, to keep myself entertained, I studied the wallpaper and traced the design with my eyes. If I had a fever, I often saw the most fantastic figures on my bedroom walls, many of them coming straight out of the fairy tales Mutti sometimes read to me when she had time, although she seldom did, which is why I always looked forward to Lenchen Oma's visits because she read to me every day while she was with us.

Sirens

I continued having problems with my tonsils, even when I got older, and Mutti always fixed me special meals when I was sick. I generally asked for boxed chicken noodle soup, chocolate pudding, soft boiled eggs and bananas, after those items became available again. All of these foods were less painful as they slid down my burning throat. I had never heard of ice cream at that time, nor was there a place to buy any, either in Allendorf or Haiger.

In later years I discovered something that had not occurred to me back then with my child's limited vision. I was not the only one who was sick all the time. There were many children who suffered illnesses during the war, mostly due to poor nutrition, and many were worse off than I. Some diseases could have been prevented or might have been less severe had there been more doctors or better medical facilities available. And there was my friend, Rosel, who got sick with scarlet fever when she was so young. The hearing loss she suffered due to this disease was permanent. Could it have been prevented with better care? Who knows if she might not have been helped had special doctors been available? Rosel, who is only a couple of months younger than I, became a good friend and, later, she taught me the sign language she was learning in a school for the deaf she attended.

*   *   *

After I outgrew my crib, Mechthild and I slept in the same room, in single beds that had been especially made to be pushed together in order to create a double bed. We had featherbeds for covers and, although they initially felt cold when we got under them, our bodies soon generated enough warmth to allow us to sleep comfortably, even without heat from a stove. In addition, Mutti always placed a copper hot-water bottle at the foot end of the beds, one for each of us, to provide extra warmth. At first these were so hot Mechthild and I had to wear crocheted bed shoes to keep from burning our feet. If I woke up during the night and touched the hot-water bottle, I could feel that it had turned lukewarm. Kicking off my bed shoes, I would soak up the last bit of warmth. However, when we woke up in the morning and stretched, accidentally touching the hot-water bottle with our bare feet in the process, we got quite a shock because it was now icy cold.

We had a small chamber pot sitting under the bed in case of emergencies. It was a long, cold walk to the bathroom down the hall and Mutti insisted we use the potty, especially when we were sick.

* * *

When I wasn't ill, Mechthild was generally put in charge of me if she wasn't in school. She had to take me with her where ever she went, because Mutti was always so busy. If Mechthild wanted to visit her friends, she had to drag me along. She recently revealed her feelings of that time to me. "Sometimes I was resentful over having to take you with me all the time and I was not always as conscientious as I should have been while I was in charge of you," she said. "One time, when you were still small enough to be in a baby buggy, it accidentally tipped over and you landed in some nettles. I should really have been more careful at that time." While nettles aren't as bad as poison ivy, the blisters they cause burn like fire and can be quite painful at first, then they itch for a couple of days. They are especially uncomfortable on a child's tender skin.

The post office and dairy were located next to each other in our small town, halfway up the hill from the school. Every morning Mutti asked Mechthild to check the mail to see if there was a letter from Papa. If I wasn't sick, I came along. I always carried a baby doll with me, one that had belonged to Mechthild when she was young enough to play with dolls. Its head was made of papier mache that was covered with a flesh-colored layer of something similar to egg shells. While we waited for the post office lady to sort through the mail, I stood there and peeled my poor dolls face just like you would an egg.

September 1942 with my favorite doll whose face got peeled on occasion.

We usually picked up our ration of milk at the same time we went after the mail, since the dairy was right next door. Mechthild carried the large milk can and I had a smaller, doll-sized one, mostly just for show. Sometimes, there wasn't any milk available. In any case, according to the ration cards, adults were only eligible for skim milk, while I had special ration card due to my young age and was allowed whole milk. The milk we took home was measured into our milk cans from huge, concrete vats. Sometimes the lady put some into my small can and it was free, no ration card required. Of course, the ration cards weren't used only for milk; there were ration cards for everything; without them people were unable to make any purchases. They were required for anything we wanted to buy such as bread, sugar, flour, even shoes and clothing, and once the stamps were used up, you did not get a chance to buy that particular product again until the next month. However, this did not mean that if you did have ration cards the item was available. Sometimes we stood in line for a long time for something we'd heard had arrived at the store that day, such as sugar or flour, only to be told when it was our turn after we'd made it to the counter, "Sorry, we're all out. Too bad; maybe next time."

Quite often the air-raid sirens went off while we were out on the street running errands for Mutti. When we heard their wailing while outside, it scared us more because we were not close to any shelter. Mechthild always grabbed me by the arm and practically lifted me up in the air and, without regard of the milk that was spilled, raced down the hill toward home and the relative safety of our basement. I usually screamed all the way because, not only was I scared of the bombs, but my arm usually hurt from the rough treatment. Sometimes we saw the planes approach over the distant hills before we made it to the front door. Thank goodness the basement door was right next to it. Mutti was usually waiting anxiously in the entrance hall for our safe return.

I didn't have much in the way of toys. Most of them were hand-me-downs from Mechthild. There were a couple of other dolls besides the one whose face I liked to peel. However, my favorite toy was a wooden Dackel (dachshund) that I could pull across the floor on its wheels. It was jointed and wiggled along behind me. I was always threatening people that it would bite them.

Another thing I can remember playing with was a box full of Mutti's buttons. "You never put them in your mouth," Mechthild told me some time ago. "But it was my job to crawl around on the floor and pick them up every time you had played with them."

*   *   *

Baths were taken on Saturday evenings. Mutti always kept the reservoir of the wood burning kitchen stove filled with water. We had running cold water, but not hot, and this way, as long as the stove was going, we had hot water available. On bath day, Mechthild brought the small, galvanized bath tub up from our special area in the basement and placed it on the stone floor of the kitchen near the stove where it was comfortably warm. This also put it close to the reservoir and the hot water did not have to be carried a great distance. Mutti then dipped the water from the reservoir into the tub, using a long-handled saucepan; she then added cold water from a bucket she'd filled beforehand at the sink, making sure the water temperature in the tub was just right. She always gave me a little time to play around in the water, although I had no tub toys. I had a wash cloth, a sponge and my hands to splash with. Since the kitchen floor was made of stone, it didn't matter if I created a few puddles. Mutti used this time to refill the reservoir. After she had scrubbed me down thoroughly, she lifted me onto the towel-covered kitchen table to dry me off. I can still hear her exclaim the words she said almost every Saturday evening back then, "Goodness, how skinny you are. I can count every one of your ribs!"

Mechthild had to use the same bathtub and water I had used, with a little hot water added. She hated that, but Mutti said it would take too long to heat more water. She, herself, used a bigger tub that she brought from the basement while Mechthild had her bath. We went into the living room while Mutti bathed. During the rest of the week we had sponge baths every morning. This was done at the kitchen sink. Although we had an indoor toilet with an overhead tank and a chain you had to pull for flushing purposes, there was no lavatory or tap in this room, nor was there any way to heat it in winter.

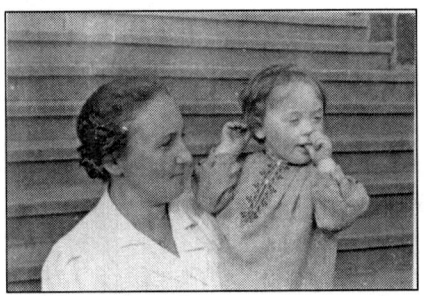

That thumb tastes so good

My childhood friend and Neighbor Hans-Ulrich

Mutti's cake sure is good

Hans-Ulrich gets to taste it too.

He bit my finger!

Sirens

Chapter 3
Mutti Keeps Busy with Her Chores

Since everything in those days had to be done by hand or from scratch as they say, even had there not been a war, doing chores took a long time, and with no men around to lend a helping hand, most women spent most of their waking hours doing some kind of work.

However, the war in Germany did make it more complicated for the housewives, in that they lacked many of the staples necessary in our daily lives such as food, heating materials and clothing, even cleaning supplies. It took extra time to procure the first two and time was needed as well to make the clothes, and it was harder to keep the house in order without the latter. Add to that the inescapable fact that people lived in continuous fear for their lives, it was not easy to try to eke out a living and live through the days in as normal a fashion as possible. Exist might actually be a better word then live. And then there were the ever-present sirens that interrupted everyday activities, and did so more and more often as the war moved toward its bitter end.

This was the reason why Mutti did not have much time to read to me, but was busy from morning until night, with her breaks spent in the basement, not resting, but waiting in terror for that first bomb to hit, then going back upstairs to continue with whatever work she'd been doing.

On winter mornings her first chore was to get a fire started in the kitchen stove, not so much for cooking, since our breakfast generally consisted of a piece of bread with whatever we could find to put on it, such as jelly or jam or some honey, but for warmth and to heat the water for our sponge baths. If there was not enough wood to build a fire in the living room stove as well, we would spend the day in the kitchen – unless I was sick. Then it was more practical to build the fire in the living room where Mutti could keep an eye on me while I was resting on the couch for the duration of my illness. We had a small, round table in that room where my mother and Mechthild ate their meals. I didn't usually feel like eating at all when my throat ached like it was on fire and when I felt feverish and weak.

Next Mutti put our apartment in order. Since the featherbeds could not be washed, they were hung out of the open windows for a short period of time to air out, summer and winter alike. This was something that could be seen all over town in the mornings because everybody used featherbeds, and one could always tell who had slept late because their windows would still be closed and their featherbeds would not be in evidence. These people were generally considered lazy. While the bedding was airing out, Mutti straightened our bedroom and the living room, picking up dirty laundry in one and books or coloring pencils or whatever we had used the night before to keep ourselves entertained from the other if we had spent the evening there. She had done her bedroom long before the rest of us woke up. She also cleaned the ashes out of the living room stove and got it ready for the next fire to be lit. (We never used the dining room.) By the time all those chores were done, it was time for her to move the bedding out of the window and make our beds.

If I was sick in bed, I liked to watch Mutti as she went about her work. It gave me something to do and relieved the boredom. This was especially the case if I was on my way to recovery and felt well enough not to want to remain in bed.

We always had our main meals at noontime, and Mutti tried to make them as interesting and as nutritious as possible. So, after the everyday housework was done, she scrounged around the pantry to see if she had anything on hand to fix for dinner. If she couldn't find anything on the shelves of the pantry, she had to go shopping. She never hesitated to leave me alone when I was sick and she had to go to the stores, although she might ring the Löber's doorbell and let them know she'd be gone for a little while, but the town was small and these trips never took very long. Also, the war and with it the bombs, were far more dangerous than whatever could befall me in our apartment. Besides, I was usually pretty good about staying put in my bed. Many people did not act the same way as they would have in peacetimes, and what else could Mutti have done with Mechthild in school.

Sometimes a trip to the butcher shop was successful and we'd have meat for dinner. But this was a rare and happy occasion. It wasn't that we lacked the money – Mutti got part of Papa's army pay – there was simply a scarcity of any kind of merchandise, especially food, available to consumers during the war.

After our meal, which was eaten by only Mutti and me since Mechthild was either in school or on her way home, my mother always expected me to take a nap, which I hated. I suppose she wanted to get me out of her hair so she could get on with her work.

My sister was usually served the leftovers from our lunch for supper while Mutti and I had sandwiches. Even if an air-raid alarm went off as soon as she arrived in Dillenburg which meant school would not be held, it still was past noon by the time she got home because she had to walk such a great distance.

Mutti washed the breakfast and lunch dishes in her enameled dishpan that she placed in the kitchen sink. She filled it half full with hot water from the reservoir, then added cold from the tap until the water in the dishpan no longer burned her hands. She never left the dishes to dry by themselves. She didn't like the messy look the dishes gave her kitchen if they were all just sitting there. They were immediately dried with a dishtowel and put away. The pots and pans, which were always black on the bottom from the stove, were dried with the dishcloth that had been wrung out. They were then set on the stove to finish drying. Sometimes, if I wasn't sick, I got to help. I pulled up a little footstool to stand on and dried the unbreakable items such as the flatware – except for the knives.

Mechthild in her Jungmädel uniform, without the tie, standing next to Mutti. I'm about two-years-old in this picture.

Saturday was always house-cleaning day. Everything was dusted and polished and scrubbed. Every other week Mutti had to scrub the stairs that led from our apartment to the front door. On the other Saturdays Frau Löber, from the apartment next to ours, had to take her turn. If we were out of soap, plain water was used. The war did not disrupt this routine, although the sirens did. When they went off, the women left in the middle of their chores and we all ran to the basement. The work was continued after the all-clear had been sounded. As the war continued, people got used to some of the inconveniences and lived as normal a life as they could. But they never got used to the danger.

In nice weather there was always some kind of work to be done in the garden, depending on the season. Mutti was proud of her gardening abilities and we often enjoyed fresh vegetables at our dinner table, although I was never very fond of spinach or beets, no matter how hungry I was. Mutti told me a story about that once, one that I could not possibly have remembered because I was still a baby.

Herr Löber had come home on leave from the war unexpectedly and Mutti had invited him and Frau Löber for dinner. Everybody was sitting around the kitchen table, and Mutti was holding me on her lap, feeding me. She had just ladled a large spoon of spinach into my mouth.

"You puffed out your cheeks," she told me, laughing at the memory, "and then you blew hard. After that everybody at the table had green freckles."

The bees, whose care Mutti had taken over from Papa, also needed attention, but not so often. The little insects caused the most work when it was time to harvest the honey.

If time allowed, Mutti chopped a little wood from the woodpile located near the beehives that were contained in a small shed. We called it the bee house.

Mutti sewed all of our clothes on a Pfaff treadle machine. She often had to use odd fabrics since those were all that were available. Generally they had ugly designs or colors. I don't know if they thought up these ugly fabric designs just because there was a war going on, but I don't see where that made any sense, although nothing about this war did. I do think the designers might have thought up something more cheerful. Mutti also had to be careful how she washed this material because it often shrank, faded, or fell apart altogether. Since I was so small, she was able to use the fabric from one or two of her old dresses to make things for me. She took them apart at the seams, and cut around any worn spots when she cut out the pattern. My mother often embellished my little dresses with embroidery or smocking to make the fabric look prettier. She even made me coats from her old ones or from those Mechthild had outgrown. In addition, I owned a number of sweaters and stockings as well as caps, scarves and mittens which she knitted in the evenings.

Mutti carries a branch she is ready to chop for firewood.

Monday was washday for us. Other families in the building washed on other days. This was a chore so time-consuming, it took up the entire day. First Mutti sorted the clothes from the hamper into piles such as whites and light and dark colors, since they had to be washed separately. The sorting was done in her bedroom where the hamper was kept. Sometimes, but not often in winter when it took longer for the clothes to dry, she added the covers from the featherbeds as well as the sheets, which made for quite a pile of laundry. I loved rolling around in the bundles of clothes. Mutti scolded me when she caught me doing this, but I did see her smile sometimes.

After the sorting was done, we had to make several trips to the basement laundry room loaded down with wicker baskets filled with dirty clothes. That is, Mutti was loaded down with clothes; I just tried not to get in the way as we both negotiated the stairs.

Now the hard work began. There were none of the modern-day appliances available that the word laundry room might suggest, not even a wringer-type washer. The room was large, with a concrete floor. In one corner sat a huge copper kettle that had been bricked up, with a fire hole at the bottom. The kettle had to be filled with cold water by means of a garden hose that was connected to a faucet. Mutti threw the white clothes into the kettle, added the soap and let them soak a bit. Sometimes she had to use shavings from hand soap if she had not been able to buy laundry soap. She immediately started a fire, using some of our wood that was stored in our basement room. Finally she placed the huge lid on the kettle and went back upstairs to do some other work such as putting fresh sheets on the beds and covers on the featherbeds and generally doing some of her usual morning work while she waited for the water in the kettle to boil. After so many years of doing this, she knew approximately how long this would take.

Once back downstairs, Mutti placed two galvanized tubs on old chairs that had been lined up against the wall, and filled them with cold water. She liked to use the chairs because they kept her from having to bend over so far.

Ursula (Winter) Turner

After the clothes had been boiling for about ten minutes she took a tool that looked somewhat like a toilet plunger but was made of copper, with a second plunger inside on a spring that allowed it to go up and down when she pushed on the wooden handle. As she stomped the plunger through the clothes with all her might, she tried to make sure she got all the dirt out of them. Often she had to take the corner of her apron, which she always wore, to wipe moisture from her face as the laundry room usually filled with steam, often so dense that I could not see Mutti even though I was playing on the floor only a few feet away. I sometimes cried when this happened because I feared I had lost her.

When she deemed the clothes clean enough, she fished them out of the kettle with a long, wooden stick that was white and worn smooth from years of use. She dropped the clothes, one by one, into the nearest tub of cold water and worked on getting the soap out of them by swishing them around for a little while. Then came the really hard part of doing laundry in this old-fashioned manner. All of the clothes, including the sheets, had to be wrung out by hand before they were dropped into the second tub to be rinsed once more. Again they had to be wrung out until not a drop of water could be forced from them. When I was older I often had to help with this and usually came away with blisters on my hands. When each piece of white laundry was as dry as possible it was dropped into a wicker basket which was set aside.

A different method was used to wash the colored clothes. Mutti emptied the two tubs into the drain hole and filled one of them with the hot, soapy water from the kettle which had cooled down some by then and no longer burned her hands. The second tub was filled with more cold water. Then she took the washboard from its hook on the wall, set it in the tub with the soapy water, and scrubbed the colored clothes, starting

Sirens

with the lighter ones, up and down the length of the corrugated metal board, again and again. When she was satisfied each garment was clean, she dropped it into the cold water in the other tub. This time the clothes were rinsed only once, but the water was changed a couple of times. These clothes also had to be wrung out. By now Mutti's hands were red and raw from the hot, soapy water and from all the scrubbing and wringing out.

If the air-raid sirens started up, all we had to do was step through the door and we were in the central shelter area.

In nice weather, the colored clothes were always hung on the clothesline that was strung along one side of the school yard. Mutti was very particular about how they were placed. Blouses were hung upside down with the clothespins at the side seams; skirts by the waist; stockings by the toes; and square or rectangular items by two corners. Since she owned few clothespins and no new ones were available at the stores, corners were often overlapped and fastened with only one pin.

White clothes had to undergo one further treatment. I don't know if bleach for clothes hadn't been invented yet or was simply not available to us, at any rate Mutti, as well as many other women, had their own system of making the clothes sparkling white. My mother used the large meadow at the bottom of the school yard, with the owner's permission, to spread all the white clothes out on the grass, making sure they were kept damp by sprinkling them with water from a watering can every so often. The sun did the rest. If they were not kept damp they turned brown. After a length of time, the clothes were gathered up again and were hung on the line from which most of the colored clothes had been removed by then since they had dried in the sun, and had been carried back up to the apartment. If the weather was inclement, all the clothes were hung in the attic which was huge, stretching from one end of the building to the other, but with divisions along the sides and at one end, just like in the basement. That end was our private part of the attic. The whites did not undergo the bleaching treatment on rainy or snowy days. Mutti was never happy about this because she felt they did not get white enough without it.

Mutti never let her ironing go, taking care of that chore the very next day. Few clothes require pressing today and electric irons make the job simple, although not many people bother to iron at all these days. However, it was quite a big chore back in the past, war or not, to get those clothes pressed and looking nice and smooth. Mutti had two heavy metal irons that had to be placed on the stove to get hot. She had no ironing board, but used the kitchen table after first a blanket, then a sheet had been spread on it. She always used the same ones and the sheet sported several scorch marks. In Mutti's opinion, almost all clothes required ironing, including her sheets and pillow cases, underwear and even the dishtowels. Using one of the irons, she left the other on the stove. When the first one turned cold, she switched to the other one. And so it went, making ironing another long-lasting, time-consuming job that was not easy since the irons were very heavy and could wear a person out.

Many of these activities were interrupted by air-raids and the sirens that gave us warning, when Mutti had to drop everything, grab me from where ever I happened to be, either playing in the kitchen or sick in bed, and rush to the basement. The danger of the bombs was always there.

I never saw Mutti write her daily letters to Papa. I'm sure she did that after I was in bed and asleep and she was more able to concentrate. But I do know that her worry about him was ever-present.

Sirens

Chapter 4
In Search of Food

I don't know what Mutti ate during her pregnancy, but I doubt she was able to lay her hands on much healthy food except for the vegetables and berries from her small garden. There wasn't a lot of any kind of food available during those dreadful times; however, if you lived in a small town as we did, with farms all around, life wasn't quite so bad. Although the farm women (the farmers had mostly gone off to war like all men) had to give up a lot of their harvest to the war effort, they sometimes had a little extra they'd secretly stashed away and they were willing to share some of that with others in need. Big-city people, on the other hand, were much worse off, with no food source nearby, and available transportation to the country almost non-existent.

Food was definitely scarce for German citizens during World War II, and the women who had been left behind by their men and were now expected to take care of their families on their own, would do just about anything to provide for their loved ones, even things that might have been embarrassing to them during normal, prewar times.

After the men in the service got their share, there was precious little left for the civilian population although the soldiers usually didn't have enough to eat either, especially toward the end of the war. Most farms missed the guiding hands of the men who were used to running them, but were now forced to play the roles of warriors, while the women, with less experience, needed extra hands to get all the work done on their farms. The best and really only resolution was therefore to make their children fill the gaps and help out. Still, the farms could not produce as much as they would have in peacetime and most of what they did produce was conscripted. And there was always the danger of air-raids to worry about while everybody was working in the fields.

Having ration cards didn't always guarantee that there would be food available for non-farm families. Although Allendorf had five grocery stores, three bakeries and two butcher shops during the war years, the shelves and store rooms of these businesses were often bare. When people saw a line form in front of any of these stores, they joined the line without even knowing what was available for purchase. It didn't matter. The point was that the store had something to sell and nobody cared what it was as long as it was something that could be put on the supper table. Food was food and you joined the line to get your share, and perhaps, if you were lucky, it was something that you could use to fix a meal with. But if you were unlucky, the store had run out of whatever it was they had for sale before you made it to the front of the line. Frustrating as this was, it was a way of life everybody had more or less gotten used to.

Mutti had a small vegetable garden on one side of the school building. A few berry bushes she had planted long before the war grew along the fence. While the bushes could be fairly well relied upon to produce berries year after year, she was not always able to grow the vegetables she normally preferred to use because the seeds were as difficult to come by as everything else.

After she'd harvested what she had grown she set to work putting them up. I always liked to watch her can her garden products such as tomatoes and pickles, and I loved the smell of the kitchen as the berries Mutti was preparing to make into jams and jellies were cooking in the pot. She always saved back whatever white sugar she'd been able to lay her hands on, in order to be able to do this. Not only did I enjoy the aroma of the cooking berries, but also the thought that there would be something good to eat for a while. Sadly there was never enough to last through the year since there was often little else to go with this food.

The few loaves of bread we were able to buy were often spoiled. We heard some people tell of cutting through a loaf (bread was never pre-sliced) and finding remnants of a mouse. This never happened to us, but we did run into mouse tracks one time in a loaf of bread. But when you're hungry, you cut around it and eat the rest.

I can remember that one of our most frequent meals consisted of potato pancakes, made from grated, raw potatoes, with applesauce to accompany them, instead of meat. Mutti always put a little dab of butter into the skillet for the first pancakes. After that was used up, she cooked the rest of them in the dry skillet. They didn't stick, but they lacked some of the flavor the ones with butter had. The applesauce was always homemade from apples we'd brought home from one of our rare forays to our grandparents farm some distance away.

When Papa had been forced to become a soldier and go to war, he left behind a number of beehives, which meant Mutti had to take on the added burden of minding the bees. The bee house, with its several colorful entrance ways for the bees, a different color for each hive (Mutti had explained that the members of each hive recognized the color of their entrance) stood on the opposite side of the school building from our garden. I sometimes showed off to my friends by stepping seemingly fearlessly into the center of a swarm of bees. What they didn't know was that these bees were males who do not sting. However, I got my come-uppance on some rare occasions when a stray female bee happened to get lost among the males and stung me. Then I'd run crying to my mother.

Getting the honey wasn't an easy job. We had a centrifuge especially made for this purpose, into which

Mutti stuck the honey combs in their wooden frames, lining them up along the outer walls. Then she cranked a handle, harder and harder, and sent the combs flying round and round until the force of the gravitational speed made the honey flow out of the combs and collect at the bottom of the machine. It then ran out of a spout and into a bucket. Later Mutti would transfer it into jars. I had fun chewing on the wax of the now-empty combs. They still contained traces of the honey, enough for me to be able to get a good taste. I did get so sick of honey eventually that I could not stand to eat it in later years, but it sure was a treat right out of the combs, especially since I was always hungry and there was so little food available. Mutti always managed to hide a few jars of the honey for our personal use, but most of it had to be turned over to the army.

Mutti also told me that the honey was the bees' food for the winter months, and we were taking it away from them. Papa had always replaced it with sugar water, using white sugar that he dissolved in hot water, which the bees were happy to feed on. However, since white sugar was seldom available during the war, and then only in small amounts, barely enough for our personal use, the army gave Mutti brown sugar to feed the bees with instead. From this she also set a small portion aside for our use. The remainder was dissolved in hot water, and I stood on my little footstool and watched Mutti as she stirred and stirred until all the sugar was liquid and the water was brown. Then she gave it to the bees who didn't seem to mind that it was only brown sugar.

We often used our brown sugar to put on bread, sort of as a sandwich spread. Since we always had open-faced sandwiches, and since there was rarely any butter or margarine available to us, the sugar did not stay well on the bread. At my young age I did not always manage to hold my slice of bread level, but tilted it every which way, and by the time I had taken a few bites, most of the sugar had landed on the table or the floor. Mutti's solution to my dilemma was to run a little tap water over the fairly solid slice of rye bread, then add the sugar, which consequently stuck nicely to the wet surface of the bread. Brown sugar was the first sweet I tasted besides Mutti's jellies and jams and, of course, the honey. I had no idea at that time what candy was or that it even existed.

During the winter months when it got dark early and no work could be done outdoors, Mutti and Mechthild spent many evenings knitting gloves and scarves from wool they had obtained by unraveling old sweaters since new wool or yarn was another item not easily available. They did the knitting by the dim light of a 25-watt bulb. Despite the black-out curtains – black material that covered the windows – no brighter light was permitted. I wasn't old enough to be of much help, but I did get to wind the unraveled yarn into a ball sometimes, or I did the unraveling while one of the others made the ball. At the age of thirteen or fourteen my big sister was becoming an excellent knitter. The items Mutti and Mechthild knitted often had fancy Scandinavian designs and were quite pretty as well as useful. Sadly, both of these women ruined their eyes doing this delicate work in such dim light.

This Verdunkelung (black-out) rule was not only followed in homes but had to be obeyed outside as well. Cars and bicycles had black rubber hoods pulled over their headlights. The hoods featured narrow slits that allowed the drivers to see a bit of the road directly in front of the vehicle. There were no streetlights.

Some women owned pins in the shape of flowers that glowed in the dark. They wore them when they had to go outside at night to keep from bumping into each other.

Outdoor programs were always scheduled for daylight hours only.

Ursula (Winter) Turner

*   *   *

After a number of the knitted items had been completed, and when our food supply was particularly low, Mutti indicated it was time to forage for some food. She hated to do this. Even though she had something to trade, she likened it to begging. But she knew we had to eat and she always bravely said, "It's time to make another trip to the country and see if we can trade our things for some food." Then she and Mechthild lugged the bicycles up the few outside steps from our basement area; any low tires were pumped full of air; and the merchandise was stowed away on the bikes with Mechthild loading up the luggage carriers at the back of the bikes, while Mutti lifted me into the child's seat that was fastened to the handlebars on her bicycle. For me these trips were fun and an adventure. We didn't get away from the house often. For the others it was hard work.

The reason for this undertaking, much as Mutti hated it, was to obtain food – whatever we could get – through trading the knitted items with area farm women. Not all farmers lived in town as they did where my parents had been raised. Some did live a little way out in the country or in very small villages. Sometimes we brought some honey along, too, because some farm women were willing to trade a pound of butter for a pound of honey. Mutti knew they made their own jellies and jams, so there was no sense in bringing any of ours especially since we ate it ourselves. But since these women were kept busy with their farms, their husbands having gone off to fight in the war, they had no time for knitting or were too tired in the evenings, and they were therefore eager to exchange butter, eggs or some meat when they had any, for gloves and scarves. If our trip had been successful, our mouths would water on the way home just thinking of the good food we'd be able to enjoy for a while.

Mutti used this bicycle when bartering for food, placing me in the child's seat.

    Sometimes, but rarely, we undertook a much longer trip. Since the train schedules were unreliable and the trains were prone to bombings, the bicycles were used even though we had some distance to cover. The place we headed for on these occasions was Launsbach, the hometown of both Mutti and Papa. On Mutti's side we only had a grandmother left. Lenchen Oma was my favorite grandparent. Her husband, Mutti's father, had died from the aftereffects of injuries he'd suffered during his service in World War I, long before I, and even Mechthild, had been born. Papa's parents, Winter Opa and Winter Oma as we called them, Winter being their and our last name, owned a small farm, and we went there not only to visit, for which the trip was much too strenuous, but because Mutti knew they would give us some food to take home. Of course we enjoyed our visits as well, although my paternal grandparents and Mutti didn't get along very well because they had been against Papa marrying her.

This trip to my parents' hometown was not easy and therefore not undertaken often. Not only was it a very long distance of 50 kilometers (about 32 miles) to be covered by a woman, a teenage girl and a small child on bicycles and on bad roads that were often pitted with bomb craters, but we were required to stop at each county line and show the special permits Mutti had had to obtain, often with difficulties, to be able to make this trip. Having these permits did not guarantee passage. If one of the guards, usually soldiers, was in a bad mood, he might actually decide not to allow us to continue our journey – but that was rare.

And then there was the ever-present danger of bombers. Out in the open countryside there were no air-raid sirens to warn us of their approach. We had to stay alert to the sound of advancing planes. *Splittergräben*, especially dug ditches, found at intervals along the sides of the road, were the only shelter available. But Mutti had her moves down pat. At the first droning sound of airplane engines approaching from the distance, she stopped her bike, grabbed me while letting the bicycle fall where it may, and leaped into the nearest Splittergraben. Mechthild followed her example. Once the planes had passed, we continued our journey.

Chapter 5
A Wartime Visit with Our Grandparents

Lenchen Oma at right, Tante Gertrud, Mechthild, and Cousin Dieter in the carriage

Although Lenchen Oma had owned a farm at one time, along with her husband, our grandfather, she gave it up after he died, because it was too much work for her to handle. However, she still lived in the farmhouse, along with Tante Gertrud, Mutti's sister, and her three little boys. She leased the land to another farm family. Therefore, Mutti could count only on her in-laws, Mechthild's and my paternal grandparents, who still owned their small farm, to give her some food to take

Ursula (Winter) Turner

home. Although Winter Opa had also fought in World War I, nothing had happened to him and he had made it home safely.

With Germany a relatively small country, farmers did not have large acreages to farm. Instead, their fields were sprinkled around the outskirts of the small towns, with a small patch here and another there, one on the other side of town, while one might be clear across the river. Since the villages are so close together, a farmer's field in Launsbach might touch on one belonging to a farmer in a neighboring town. Most of the farmers could not make a living at farming alone and had to find a day job elsewhere while the women saw to the livestock and the farming was often done in the evenings and on weekends.

Winter Opa is standing next to the hay wagon that has the two milk cows hitched to it.

There was no machinery to do the farm work. Our grandparents, as did most of the farmers, owned two milk cows that also served to pull the wagons, as they carried potatoes, turnips, grain or hay, and they pulled the plow and other farm equipment as well. My grandparents also raised two pigs each year and some chickens and ducks. During the war they didn't get to keep much of the result of their hard labor since most was confiscated by the army just like the harvest of all the other farmers. However, Winter Opa was too old for this war and was allowed to remain home and work his farm. He did hold a second job for a while, and also received a pension from his service in the First World War.

Winter Opa plows while Tante Maria leads the cows.

Winter Oma's and Opa's two and a half story house was located in town. It occupied a corner lot, with the barn about half a block down the street. Between these two buildings, at the back of the yard, you found first, next to the barn, the pig pen, then the manure pile, the outhouse, a couple of sheds, and finally, next to the house, the summer kitchen. All of these structures were one story tall and touched on each other, but were otherwise not connected except for the summer kitchen which had an entrance to the cellar that could also be reached from the house by way of a set of very steep, curved stairs. Both the barn and the house stretched up to the street, while the other buildings ran along the back of the lot. A courtyard, paved with uneven cobblestones, filled the remaining space to the street. A fence with one big gate for the wagon and a small one to be used by people bordered the sidewalk. The wagon and other farm tools such as the plow and disc were stored in the yard next to the barn.

I sort of liked Winter Oma, although she was not the kind of person you ran up to and hugged. She was too formidable for that. To me she seemed a large woman who usually wore the ankle length, somber-colored skirts of the time, voluminous and gathered at the waist. I kept my distance from Winter Opa. Having fought in the war must have done something to his mind unless he had always been this way which I had no way of knowing but was afraid to ask about. When I looked at his face, something I tried to avoid doing, it always made me think he had bitten into something sour or bitter. I don't think I ever saw him smile. It was obvious he didn't like children. He never talked to my cousins or me unless he growled about something we'd done to displease him. I hated to sit across from Winter Opa at the dinner table because he always got food lodged in his huge, bushy mustache when he ate. And napkins were not something used during those days, at least not at a farmer's dinner table.

Besides our grandparents, our aunt, Papa's sister Johanna and her son Wolfgang also lived in the house. Tante Johanna was never addressed by her name. She was Mechthild's Got (godmother, pronounced like mode) and since my sister was the oldest of the grandchildren, all the rest of us, our cousins and I, as we came along, heard Mechthild call her Got, and consequently imitated her and did the same. She remained Got, even to people of the village who were not related, until the day she died. Her husband and older son both fought in the war. I never met them because they did not come home when the war was over, but were declared missing and were never found. They are both probably buried somewhere in Russia.

Got and her remaining son, Wolfgang

On our food foray visits to Launsbach, I liked to play in the courtyard of my grandparents' farm when the weather was nice. Mutti knew I was as safe there as was possible with the buildings on three sides and the fence on the fourth – except from the bombers. Nobody was safe from them and they could get you anywhere. So, she always told Mechthild to keep an eye on me while she was busy helping Winter Oma with whatever work needed to be done during our visit.

One year we went for two visits, one not too long after the other and my cousin Wolfgang remembers both very clearly.

"It must have been in fall of 1944," he said. "Winter Oma and Opa, my mother, you and I were sitting in the summer kitchen at the supper table." Evidently Mutti and Mechthild were visiting our other grandmother. "Suddenly the air-raid sirens sounded," he continued, "and we should have rushed to the cellar. But you were making such funny faces that everybody burst out laughing and continued watching you and we completely forgot about the alarm."

For the second visit Mutti had decided to take a chance and go by train for once since it was during winter and quite cold. I think she wanted to spend Christmas in her hometown because she was particularly worried about Papa since she had not heard from him in a long time. During this visit we had the most horrifying experience that I can remember from the war.

I was playing in a little bit of snow that had come down earlier on this day, in my favorite corner of the yard, when the air-raid sirens started up their howling once again. Mutti was visiting her mother, our Lenchen Oma. Mechthild and our cousin Wolfgang were standing at the gate to the yard, watching as the planes flew overhead. They were not worried, thinking that all these planes could not possibly mean to drop their bombs on the small town of Launsbach, but were instead headed for the big city of Gießen, not far away, to do their damage there.

"It was Christmas Eve 1944," Wolfgang recalls, "a clear winter day with a little dusting of snow covering the ground. While we were standing at the gate watching as the bombers flew across the sky above our heads we suddenly heard a hissing and roaring sound. We knew immediately – those were bombs dropping from the planes!"

The village of Launsbach

Nobody seems to know the reason why so many bombs were dropped onto such a small town, although some of the citizens of Launsbach suspect that the Flak in Gießen was shooting at the planes as they came closer to the city, and the pilots were trying to get rid of their dangerous loads before they got hit. Not wanting to waste the bombs altogether, they dropped them on the little town.

Mechthild grabbed my hand and we all hurried toward the cellar by way of the front door. Although the route through the summer kitchen would have been closer, the older children evidently panicked and chose the longer route.

"We didn't get very far before we heard a loud detonation nearby," said my cousin. "Glass shards from the front door, which we were trying to reach, were flying around our ears. About 50 to 60 or more bombs fell that evening, some only about 100 yards away."

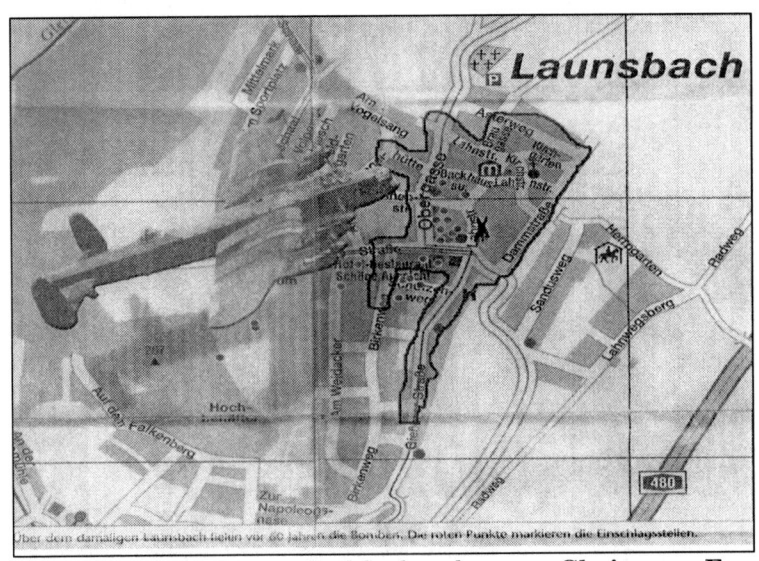

Launsbach was attacked by bombers on Christmas Eve 1944. Each black dot indicates a hit by a bomb.

One of the pieces of glass hit me in the nose, causing it to bleed profusely. At my age, I had no conception of what a bomb actually was, but in my young mind I just knew that a piece of a bomb had got me. When I saw all the blood that was dripping down the front of my dress I started to scream at the top of my lungs, "A bomb has hit me in the nose; a bomb has hit me in the nose!" By the time we made it down to the bottom of the basement stairs, the people assembled there, my grandparents, and Got, who had been in the summer kitchen and had entered the cellar from that direction, all knew I'd been hit by a bomb.

Since Mutti was at her mother's house, Got took me on her lap and the large man's handkerchief she always carried mercifully put a stop to the bleeding, although the cut did hurt for a while and the "bomb" left a bruise. From that day on I considered myself a casualty of the war. After that incident, I was always one of the first to run to the cellar when the sirens started their wailing.

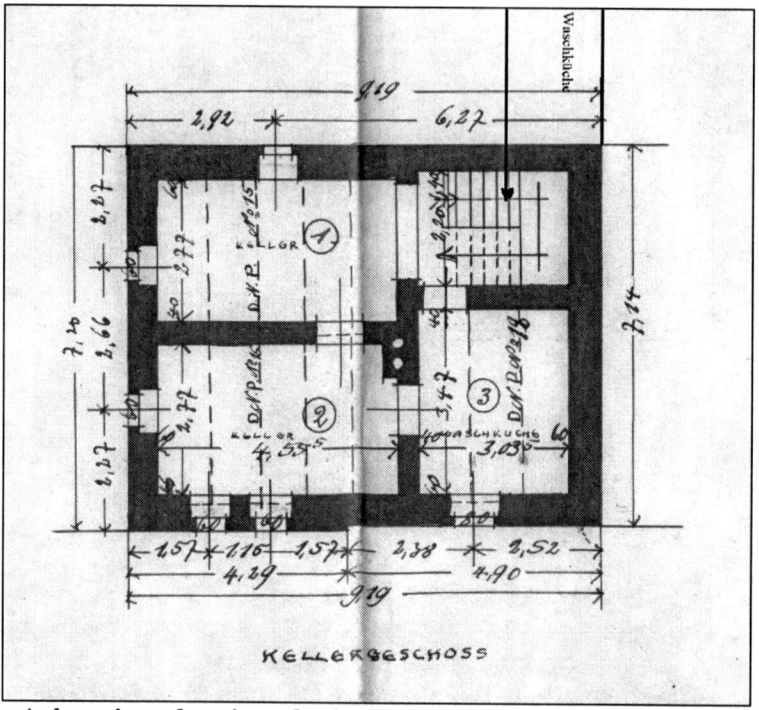

A drawing showing the basement in my grandparents' house where we went when the sirens sounded. Room No. 1 was the shelter room. The other rooms were used for storage.

*   *   *

My cousin, Dieter, Tante Gertrud's oldest son, has his own story to tell. For several years, from 1943 until the end of the war, when he was between eight and ten years old, he regularly went to the fields and woods with his buddies. "We often saw American bomb squads fly overhead and also some low flying fighter planes. They were so close sometimes that we could see the pilots in the cockpit."

For over a year, from March 2, 1944 to March 27, 1945, the citizens of Gießen had to suffer through 28 bombing assaults. While the English attacked at night, the American bombers did their damage during the day.

Dieter remembers that the attacks always followed a certain pattern. "First they threw flares," he said. "High explosive bombs came next to cause the buildings to collapse, followed by other bombs that set everything on fire that was left. These were mixed with bombs containing timers in order to hamper attempts to extinguish the fires."

My cousin did experience the huge bombing attack on Gießen on December 6, 1944, although from a distance. "Afterward we ran to the train station in Launsbach from where we could see the city burn from one end to the other," he recalls.

In the end, this attack on Gießen caused about 60 percent of the city to be destroyed. Only 3,000 apartments remained undamaged. More than 800 citizens lost their lives. The assault was initiated by British bombers.

Dieter explained that he is not aware of any photographs that might exist of the air-raid on Launsbach. "Most people didn't own a camera," he said, "and those who did had no film." Evidently it had been forbidden by the Hitler regime to take any pictures of the destruction Germany was suffering from the bombings. "Our mother had a camera, but no film," said Dieter. "When the American soldiers occupied Launsbach and made a house-to-house search, they found our camera and took it with them. But I think some people managed to take pictures anyway," he added.

The Liebig Schule was bombed toward the end of the war. Cousin Dieter was a student there.

My cousin remembers a small airfield that was located a few miles east of Launsbach that was used by German fighter planes which did a lot of flying during the last days of the war. With the bomb squads being escorted by smaller planes as well, a lot of aerial fights broke out with many of the planes being shot down on both sides. Many of these planes crashed, with their pilots still in the cockpit, and buried themselves deep into the ground.

In later years a group of Germans made it their mission to find these crash sites and to dig the planes up. This allowed them to identify a number of the pilots, by checking their dog tags or by other means, and notify their relatives. The relatives then were able to give their loved ones a decent burial

These pilots were either German, American or English and most of them had been declared as missing.

*   *   *

Ursula (Winter) Turner

While at the farm, we ate fairly well, although some of the meals Winter Oma fixed were odd, to say the least. With so many people to feed, she had to throw together what she could find, enough to try to fill everybody up, and she came up with some strange combinations. Many of the meals were meatless since my grandparents, too, had to give their share to the men in the service. One of the strangest meals I can remember eating at my grandmother's house consisted of fried potatoes and Dickmilch (milk that had been allowed to curdle – on purpose). The Dickmilch was served in shallow soup bowls, ladled on top of the greasy potatoes, with sugar sprinkled on top of that. When I think of it now, it sounds awful, but at the time it was filling, although not very nutritious, and kept us from being hungry. Most of us were happy to fill our bellies with just about anything edible that could accomplish that.

When we returned home to Allendorf, we always carried something in the baskets and bags we had brought with us. If we got potatoes and a few apples, I was always happy because I knew Mutti would make potato pancakes and applesauce, one of my favorite meals, even to this day. It didn't occur to me that some people might expect some kind of meat to be served along with this. Mutti always fixed this combination as a complete meal, even long after the war was over when meat was readily available again, and that was just fine with me; and Papa liked it, too, after he came home. The only difference was that Mutti would add more butter or some kind of oil when the skillet ran dry.

I was always glad to get back home after seeing our grandparents so I could visit with my friends again. There was nobody to play with at my grandparents' house. Wolfgang was too old for me – closer to Mechthild's age – and Mutti didn't let Mechthild take me to my other grandmother's house to give me a chance to play with those cousins who were closer to my age. Because of the constant air-raids she wanted us to stay at Winter Opa's because she felt their cellar shelter was safer. I didn't think so. I preferred the safety of our own basement at home. I had never been hit by any "bomb" there.

Ursula (Winter) Turner

Chapter 6
A Trip to the Forest

The town of Allendorf looks down into a long, narrow valley, with the school building near the bottom and the houses of the village rising up along the hill behind it. The ground continues to rise beyond the last houses with, first, fields, which have been bisected by an interstate highway since I lived there, then the forest taking over. The valley on the other side of the school is split by a small creek, the *Haigerbach*, with the highway on the other side of that. Then the land ascends again, featuring more fields and more woods that make up the landscape. Halfway up, between some of the fields the railroad tracks can be seen along the hillside before they disappear among the trees. The town's cemetery is located between the road and the train tracks. We were able to look down on the creek and all that lay beyond it from Mutti's back bedroom windows as well as from the ones in the living room.

The view we had from the opposite side of our apartment through the kitchen windows went no farther than two streets as they merged into a V-shape on the left of our building. The street directly in front of the school ran level and was, logically, called *Schulstraße*. The other part of the V climbed steeply out of sight due to a sharp curve. My friend Elsa and her family lived in a house directly across from us on the steep street which was called *Scheidstraße*. We could not see anything beyond that except for a few tall trees that towered among the houses we knew were there.

If I climbed to the attic and looked in the same direction, I could see over the roofs of the houses to the steep hill beyond the town, to the fields, and then the forest.

We visited these woods quite often.

Sirens

When the time came that the little pile of fire wood in our corner of the basement had shrunk down to practically nothing because the branches Mutti had chopped up earlier had to be used in the cook stove in the kitchen as well as to heat the living room, and also for doing the laundry and therefore didn't last long, preparations were made to get some more. Since we rarely were able to get coal, we had to use wood for cooking and heating – wood that we had to procure for ourselves.

In wintertime we always followed the same procedure. Mechthild took me into our room and bundled me up until I could barely move. This was supposed to keep me from catching another one of my colds or from coming down with tonsillitis again. Then she, too, put on her warmest clothes.

In the meantime Mutti, who had put on her winter things earlier, brought our little, hand-pulled wagon out from the basement. Once outside, she attached the ladder sides Papa had made before he left. This made the cart taller, allowing it to hold more of anything we loaded into it. She'd also grabbed a couple of burlap sacks and placed them into the bottom of the cart.

After we met on the street in front of the building, I climbed into the wagon and sat down on the sacks, then Mechthild and Mutti got hold of the wagon's handle and pulled it up the Scheidstraße toward the forest. We could have taken a different road other than the part of the V we ascended, but the forest was farther away on that one and we would be exposed longer to any possible bombing attacks and, although there were some bunkers dug into the steep banks alongside this road to be used for bomb shelters, Mutti preferred to use the closer road that ran between the houses and finally to the woods. Once we had reached the trees, we were out of sight from any bombers that might approach from any direction.

The ground among the trees was always covered with branches that had been knocked down by storms or had fallen due to old age. Those branches were what we had come for. As soon as we had found a good spot among the trees, my mother and sister parked the wagon and got busy gathering up as much of the brushwood as the wagon would hold. Mutti had brought a small axe along and used it to chop up the larger ones to a more manageable size.

In the meantime my job was to pick up pinecones off the ground and put them into the burlap sacks. The trees in this part of the woods were mixed – some pines and several species with foliage such as oak and maple – so we were able to get what we had come for, good branches as well as the pinecones which Mutti liked to use for kindling.

When the cart was loaded with as many branches as it would hold, Mutti and Mechthild helped me finish filling the sacks with the pinecones. These were tossed on top of the load of wood. It was a good thing that the road toward home was all downhill since the cart was quite heavy now. Mutti took the handle and walked in front, sometimes having a difficult time keeping the cart from running her over. Mechthild walked alongside with her hand on the sacks to keep them from falling off, while at the same time trying to hold the wagon back to help slow it down a little. I trotted behind the cart, doing the best I could to keep up on my short legs which was made more difficult by all the cumbersome clothes I was wearing. I remember complaining all the way because I didn't get to ride on the cart this time.

Once back home Mechthild carried and I dragged one sack each of the pinecones to the basement. Then we all helped unload the branches from the wagon into the corner of the school yard near the bee house where a chopping block was set up permanently. The final job was Mutti's who had to chop the branches into pieces that would fit into the stoves. She didn't do this all at once but over a period of several days as she found time for this chore.

Mutti chops the wood we brought from the forest into smaller pieces.

Mechthild and I carried the shortened pieces into the basement in baskets. This took numerous trips, but we were glad of the work because we knew we wouldn't have to freeze for a while, and the wood would also be used for cooking our often skimpy meals. But we all knew another such trip would eventually become necessary. In summer, when we didn't need any wood for heating and only used it for cooking and doing laundry, we didn't have to make so many trips to gather wood, but we went there for another reason.

During the warm summer months we made several excursions up the steep hill beyond our town without the cart, carrying containers instead to hold the wild blueberries we intended to pick. Mutti usually used the large milk can, Mechthild had a big tin can that had been fitted with a wire handle, and I brought my small milk can, without the lid, because Mutti said she was sure I would lose it. We were always delighted when we found a patch of blueberries under the trees. I quickly learned that the berries that grew in the shade under the trees were much larger than the ones that saw more sunlight. However, despite picking only the larger berries, it still took me a long time to fill my container because I managed to put more berries into my mouth than what found their way into my milk can, and a big part of my face around my mouth was purple and blue by the time we returned home. Mutti had to do quite a bit of scrubbing under loud protestations on my part to get my face clean. That berry juice was stubborn and refused to come off.

We don't bake pies in Germany, but even if she lacked a few of the ingredients, the next day Mutti always baked the best blueberry cake even with the limited supplies she had on hand. And the blueberry jam she made later was delicious on my slice of bread, which I didn't have to worry about watering down to keep the jam from falling off, even without butter or margarine.

*   *   *

One of my mother's cousins, whom we considered our aunt and therefore called her Tante Dorle, lived in the big city of Frankfurt. She was in constant fear of losing her life since that city was targeted regularly by the bombers.

She told us on one of her visits, "When the air-raid sirens sound, people throughout Frankfurt rush for their shelters and hunker down, listening for the airplane engines and hoping they will pass overhead quickly without dropping their deadly loads onto the city." She continued, "As soon as the raids are over and the sirens sound the all-clear, everybody comes out from their shelter to survey the damage."

Sirens

Some discovered that their homes had been demolished right above their heads while they were sitting in the basement. Others fared even worse by finding dead relatives and neighbors. Yet others, like Tante Dorle, were lucky and found their houses still standing.

The Allies showered German cities with a rain of death, such as incendiaries or delayed action bombs, causing anything to burn that had not already been destroyed by the force of the falling bombs.

"After all this time people are getting used to this way of living," said Tante Dorle, "and they are adjusting their day-to-day living as best as they can. But it's nice to get away from it all and spend some time with family in the country," she added. She knew we, too, went to the basement a lot, but she also knew that we had never been bombed and were less likely to be targeted than big cities.

Tante Dorle, trying to get away once in a while from the constant danger, came to visit us as often as she could, whenever the trains ran, and often would arrive unexpectedly, along with her little son. She usually stayed for an extended period of time. Toward the end of the war she became a permanent visitor until no more bombs were being dropped. Her husband was also away fighting in the war. He never returned.

One Sunday afternoon, she and Mutti decided to forget about the war and all its problems, and also to forget about their husbands who were fighting in this senseless war, even if only for a little while, and go for a leisurely walk in the woods. While the others strolled along under the cool shade of the trees, enjoying the chirping of the many birds and the fresh scent of pine, I ran back and forth, picking up extra large pine cones or trying to spy a rabbit or deer. But I soon grew tired from all the running. We had walked a little farther than we normally did when we went after wood or berries. Just as I was ready to begin whining about my legs being tired and wanting to be carried, we stumbled onto a clearing.

It appeared as though this area had been used by wood cutters who evidently had abandoned their project to go fight in the war. Tree trunks as well as boards were stacked to one side, while others were still lying around, helter skelter. While we sat on one fairly thick trunk to rest and eat the sandwiches and drink the water the adults had brought along, Tante Dorle had an idea. The two women carried one of the boards to the tree trunk we'd been sitting on and laid it across its width – and just that quickly we had a ready-made see-saw. Tante Dorle and her son Jürgen sat at one end of the board and Mutti placed me in front of her on the other end. The weight was a little uneven, but we made it work and see-sawed merrily for a while, enjoying a wonderful moment for a small space of time, while forgetting about the terrible war going on all around us.

By the time we returned home, Oma had set the table with sandwich fixings for our supper.

This is one of the more joyous incidents I recall from my early childhood.

After supper the adults all sat around the radio in the living room, trying to find out what was going on with the war, while Jürgen and I played on the floor and Mechthild went to the kitchen to do some homework.

The Nazis forbade the listening of foreign radio stations and had the populace so cowed that most obeyed this rule. An atmosphere of mistrust and fear was spread and no one dared say anything against the Nazis in case they were heard and reported, just as neighbors could report you if you did not fly the flag on the days the Nazis decreed you should. Not showing the flag on those days was cause for imprisonment.

What we were able to get on German radio was mostly propaganda and one never knew how much of that was true. Consequently, many Germans were at a loss of what was happening in their world. That's why so many of the German population never heard of the concentration camps until after the war was over unless they lived in the vicinity of one, and even then many villagers weren't sure exactly what was going on inside.

Mutti and I on the see-saw we made from a wooden plank we found in a forest clearing.

*   *   *

My mother, grandmother, Tante Dorle, and later Mechthild when she was done with her homework, usually ended up playing cards or a board game, with the radio turned off.

Chapter 7
Mechthild Goes to School

In Germany children start high school after they complete the fourth grade, when they are about ten years old, but they must pass a test. Consequently Mechthild no longer attended the classes below our apartment. Being the daughter of a teacher, she was expected to attend high school, which not all of the German students did with other alternatives available to them. My sister did pass the test and now had a much longer trek to school. She had to walk 2 kilometers (about 1 ¼ mile), carrying a heavy school bag, to the neighboring town of Haiger, where the nearest railroad station was located at the other end of town. Allendorf was not considered large enough to rate a station. From Haiger she took the train another 7 kilometers (about 4 ½ miles) to Dillenburg, the county seat, where she attended the high school nearest to us at that time. She would have much preferred to go to school in Haiger, where I later went, but that school was not open during the war. To make it a little easier, she could have taken her bicycle to the train station, but would have had to leave it there and it would not have been safe from thieves.

This walk to Haiger and the subsequent train ride might not seem like such a big deal. Many students in America used to walk that distance, or more, to attend school every day – but not while they had to worry about bombers with their deadly cargo suddenly appearing overhead. Once on the train there was even more danger since the railroads in particular were a prime target for the enemy, with either the tracks or the trains being bombed to cut off supply lines.

Sirens

Mechthild remembers, "Once a low-flying plane strafed the train I was riding in and shot and killed the engineer."

Dillenburg was a larger town and, since it was also the county seat, the city was bombed regularly. Often the air-raid sirens went off not long after my sister had arrived at her school and all students were immediately ushered to a long hallway in the school building's basement where they waited out the air-raid on benches along the walls. As soon as the all-clear was sounded the students were allowed to leave the basement, but they did not return to their classrooms because school was generally dismissed for the day after an air-raid, no matter what time of day it was. Trains did not run for some time either, even after the all-clear announced that it was supposedly safe again. This meant Mechthild, along with several fellow students, had to undertake that long trip home on foot.

Several students lived in towns along the way where they left the highway and headed for their homes. Others walked with her as far as Haiger, but after they reached that town she was on her own. This meant she had to walk the entire 9 kilometers (5 ½ miles) under constant threat of bombs, with the last two kilometers all by herself. Nevertheless, Mutti insisted Mechthild continue attending school. After all, education was important and Papa would expect her to go. What she didn't seem to realize was that my sister wasn't leaning much under these conditions, particularly with her school closed so often.

Some part of their journey was through woods where the students felt relatively safe since they could not be seen from the sky while under the trees. But other parts were out in the open and the children felt exposed and were afraid, remaining alert and ready to drop into one of the *Splittergräben* which had been dug along the road at regular intervals for the explicit purpose of using them as protection from approaching planes.

One time, after they had made it close to Haiger but were still under some trees, the girls could hear the droning sound of plane engines in the distance. Soon several bombers came into view and got larger and larger. When they had reached the train station which was located at the side of town from which the girls were approaching, they dropped their load of bombs and quickly disappeared.

Moving carefully toward the scene of the disaster, Mechthild and her friends had to make their way carefully around fresh bomb craters and step cautiously over downed electric wires. The railroad overpass had been damaged, making it nearly impossible for the girls to reach the other side, but after climbing over piles of rubble, and around spark-spitting cables, they finally made it. It could have been worse for them. Had they been a little bit faster on their way home and had they arrived an instant sooner, they would have been hit by the bombs and would probably not have survived.

Soon the other students veered off the main street to go to their homes while Mechthild, her heart still racing in her chest, had to walk another 2 kilometers before arriving at home. She was never so relieved as when she was able to close the door to our apartment behind her on this eventful day.

She had been lucky, but a friend who lived too far from the school to walk home always had to wait until the trains ran again. One time her train was attacked by low-flying fighter planes and Mechthild's friend was shot. "She didn't come back to school and I never heard from her again," said Mechthild. "I never learned whether she died from her wounds or if her parents simply kept her home from school after this happened. Many students did not attend school during the war, especially toward the end, but with Papa being a teacher, Mutti insisted I get an education one way or another."

We were more aware of the destruction the bombs were doing to Haiger, Gießen and Frankfurt because we lived or had relatives in or near those cities.

But a number of other cities received unbelievable damage due to the air strikes. The city of Würzburg had only three houses left that remained intact after a bombing attack. Everything else in this city was destroyed within a 20-minute time span. This city was over 1,300 years old. But all that remained of the ancient buildings, besides those three, was ashes. The firestorm caused by incendiary bombs destroyed all of its history.

Other cities fared as badly or worse. Dresden, Cologne and Hamburg were three of the worst hit cities in Germany during World War II, especially Dresden. On the night of February 13, 1945, Britain's Royal Air Force dropped over 2,700 tons of bombs onto this baroque city which was known as "Florence of the Elbe," turning it into a wasteland of rubble and charred corpses. American bombers followed up the attack with two daytime raids on February 14 and 15.

The bombs dropped by the British onto this medieval city, the seventh largest in Germany, which normally had a population of about 650,000, but now had an uncountable number of people staying there who were war refugees, fleeing from the ever advancing Red Army of the Russians, were incendiary bombs that were filled with chemicals such as magnesium, phosphorus or napalm.

Dresden had not had a single air strike, until that particular bombing attack and was, because of this, virtually undefended.

And while the Allies put the death toll at about 35,000, some German sources of the time claimed at least 100,000 had been victims of the firestorm.

Ursula (Winter) Turner

*   *   *

When Mechthild was not in school or taking care of me, she attended meetings of the Jungmädel (young girls) group which was not optional. She was drafted into this group. It was compulsory for every girl between the ages of ten and fourteen to become a member and attend these meetings. After that age girls moved up to BDM or Bund der Deutschen Mädel for girls age fifteen to eighteen, the female version of the all male Hitler Youth.

Mechthild in her Jungmädel uniform

We met a couple of times a week," Mechthild explained. "We either did gym or sang songs, or we did some crafts, making toys for families with lots of children. Hitler liked it when people had many children, especially if they were boys, since they would become future soldiers."

Sirens

To be eligible for either of the girls' groups, future members had to be ethnic Germans, German citizens and free of hereditary disease. Mechthild was expected to attend all social evenings and sporting events. After she turned fourteen, my sister had to attend a meeting in another town to learn her duties for the BDM. She hated this and was happy when the war ended before she turned fifteen when she no longer had to worry about any of Hitler's orders.

The girls' uniform consisted of a dark blue skirt, a white blouse and a black neckerchief that was held together with a leather slide that looked like a knot. Mechthild still has her slide. She kept it as a memento and in order to never forget how bad her growing up years had been and to, some day, show it to her children and grandchildren and tell them all about her war experiences.

In truth, there was nothing else to entertain young people except for the Hitler Youth meetings and all they entailed.

The young men and women literally had their youth taken away from them as there were no dances or other forms of light entertainment. Hitler did not think it proper for people to have fun while the country's men were being slaughtered on the battlefields.

This war was bringing misery to the little people of Germany, those who were innocent of any crime and who just wanted to live in peace, but had to suffer instead. And even small children, who didn't know what was going on around them and who were not aware that there might have been a different kind of life for them, had it not been for this war that a man named Hitler had started, never had a real childhood. And many were left with mental scars due to the events they experienced during their formative years as well as physical problems because of bad nutrition during their youth.

Ursula (Winter) Turner

Chapter 8
Oma and Mechthild go after Medicine

Toward the end of the war Mutti's mother, our Lenchen Oma, decided to come for another visit, partly to give Mutti a helping hand with all her chores and partly to spend some time with her older daughter and her granddaughters. She came by train, which was an uncertain way to travel at the time because you never knew if the trains would run. It was also a dangerous mode of travel since trains were so often targeted to be bombed. This time Oma was destined to spend some time with us because many of the trains that did run were carrying troops from or to the front, and there was no room for civilians.

Lenchen Oma was very different from Winter Oma. She was warm and kind and she liked children very much. She was also short, like Mutti. And she was poor. Mechthild and I always looked forward to her visits and, although the train station wasn't very safe either, the three of us, Mutti, Mechthild and I, always made the 2-kilometer trek to meet our Oma and to help her carry her bags.

I was particularly happy when Oma came to visit because, unlike my mother, my Lenchen Oma made time for me, and she read to me every evening. Mutti was always too busy and, in retrospect, I can understand why, but I did not comprehend at that time why she so seldom read my favorite stories to me. I'm also certain that Mechthild, even though she had been given the privilege of giving me my name which she chose from a popular song of the time (as did thousands of others), got a little fed up with having to take care of me all the time. I was convinced of this after I heard of the incident with the nettles which I had been too young to remember at the time, but which had been told to me

Sirens

by a meddling neighbor lady since then. So my sister was always glad when Oma arrived and took charge of me. This was understandable. After all, she was still a child herself.

When Lenchen Oma visited, she slept in our room. I looked forward to sleeping in the same bed with my big sister while Oma took over my bed. However, when the bombing got really bad and one air-raid followed another, Mutti "slept" on the couch in the living room and made up a make-shift bed for me in that room as well. And we all slept with our clothes on. Interruptions to our sleep were the norm now and there were times when we had to rush to the basement as many as five times in a single night.

The only thing that bothered me about Oma's visits was her loud snoring – and it was loud. There was no getting away from that. I think that was why she slept with us instead of in Mutti's room where Papa's side of the bed stood empty. Mutti needed her rest so she could take care of all the work waiting for her each day.

*   *   *

One morning, during one of Oma's visits, Mutti woke up with a painful rash all over her face. She didn't know what had caused it, but knew that her skin was quite sensitive and that she was also very susceptible to insect bites, so the rash could have been caused by a number of things. In those days, even before the war, people didn't visit their doctor for what they considered minor ailments. Although there was an elderly doctor still practicing medicine in Haiger, too old to go to war, Mutti did not consult him.

After seeing our mother's face, our neighbor, Frau Löber, suggested a salve she had used for a similar ailment. Since there was no drugstore in Allendorf, this called for a trip to the *Apotheke* (pharmacy) in Haiger.

Ursula (Winter) Turner

Allendorf didn't have much of anything really, including a police station.

It was decided that Oma and Mechthild would walk to Haiger to get the salve. Mechthild was home from school because the trains weren't running again. She might as well have stayed home for good as many times as she had to walk home from school, but Mutti wouldn't hear of it. Oma didn't know how to ride a bike or she could have used Mutti's, but they didn't mind the walk, as long as the bombers stayed away.

When the two of them arrived at their destination and asked for the salve, they discovered to their dismay that the pharmacist was unable to give them any because he only stocked it in a large container and customers were required to bring their own small ones to carry the salve home in. Neither Oma nor Mechthild had been aware of this. They hated the thought of having walked all this way for nothing, but were stumped as to what they could do.

After some deliberation while standing on the sidewalk in front of the *Apotheke*, Mechthild suddenly remembered that Mutti had a friend who lived in Haiger, a little distance from the pharmacy. So she and Oma started toward "Tante" Bertha's house to see if she might loan them a container into which they could have the pharmacist scoop the salve. However, as so often happened anymore, they didn't make it very far before the air-raid sirens commenced with their piercing wails. Their visit to Tante Bertha's house had to be detoured to the nearest shelter, which they found in the nick of time at the last warning sound of the sirens.

Haiger's Lutheran Church sits on top of a hill which is perforated with catacombs that were now being used as bomb shelters. Oma and Mechthild, along with numerous others, seeking a safe place in which to spend the time during yet another raid, hurried through the entrance of this shelter that they expected to protect them from the deadly bombs. Unlike Allendorf, Haiger

Sirens

was often targeted by the bombers so, if the sirens went off, there was a good chance that bombs would be dropped.

During all this time Mutti was waiting at home, worried sick about her mother and her daughter. She had heard the sirens as they were sounded in Haiger and she had also heard the planes as they approached the neighboring town. And she heard the bombs as they screamed down from the planes and exploded into homes, businesses and the ground. Before long she saw smoke rise toward the sky from the beleaguered town. And she worried and wondered if she would ever see her loved ones again.

It was dark by the time the two women were permitted to leave the shelter of the church's underground caves, arriving home exhausted, hungry and without the salve. "We had to sit in those dark cellars for almost six hours," Mechthild told us excitedly almost as soon as they'd walked through the door, safely home from their ordeal. "We had to watch a lot of wounded people being carried past us on stretchers," my sister continued. "That's how we knew that a lot of bombs must have hit. It was awful! I was so scared!"

Although they had tried to leave several times because they knew Mutti would be worried, the air-raid wardens at the entrance would not allow them to leave the shelter until the all-clear had sounded, which did make sense.

Lenchen Oma continued the story, "Bertha's house received a direct hit during the raid, but they found her alive, although hurt, in a hole in the basement. We happened to walk past her house on our way home. Her legs had been crushed by a fallen beam."

They found out later, that a bomb had also fallen in front of the *Apotheke*, exactly onto the spot where the two of them had stood not long before while deciding what to do about getting a container for the salve.

Ursula (Winter) Turner

I don't know if Mutti ever got her salve. I suppose somebody went the next day with a container and picked some up. Life had to go on, and in those days people were forced to take chances if they wanted to continue on if only in a semblance of normal living.

By this time, both the fighting and the bombings had accelerated. Although we didn't know it yet, the war was nearing its end. Since the trains in particular were not safe and had no regular schedules anyway, Lenchen Oma's visit with us lasted for several months this time, until the war was over and some time beyond that.

Sirens

Chapter 9
Ethnic Germans Flee Eastern Europe

At the time of the outbreak of World War II, Eastern Europe was a melting pot of Russians, Ukrainians, Germans, Poles, Czechs and Dutch, to name just a few. When at home, these Germans, as well as the others, spoke in their own language, but away from home, many Germans spoke Russian along with the other languages represented in the area where they lived. These people had been living there for so long that not one of those who had actually been born in Germany was left.

When, in September 1939, Nazi Germany invaded Poland, followed by Russia invading eastern Poland, the country was divided in half by Hitler and Stalin. The two dictators also signed a non-aggression pact called the Ribbentrop-Molotov pact, named after the foreign ministers of the two countries. A part of this pact dealt with Russia's undesirables, the millions of ethnic Europeans who lived in the Soviet Union. A deal was agreed upon that allowed German and Dutch speaking people to be sent back to their countries of origin. These people had no choice in the matter. Although they had never lived in these countries and spoke mostly in their own dialect, an offshoot of German, they had to leave what they considered their home.

Also at this time many of the ethnic Germans found themselves being deported to Siberia, and few came back.

Those families who were repatriated were given a list of items they could take with them. This list was very short and they had to leave most of their personal belongings behind in the Soviet Union.

Then came the betrayal. These people had been forced to leave what they considered their rightful homes but had been told they would receive property of equal value when they arrived in the West. But they never made it there. Hitler decided to settle them in a region of the recently conquered Poland instead.

Another area greatly affected by evacuations in 1944 and 1945 was Preußen (Prussia) and Pommern (Pomerania). The evacuation of Ostpreußen (East Prussia) began because the citizens feared the advancing Soviet army who, by then, was fighting against Germany. Many of the refugees took to the roads voluntarily just to get away from the Russian soldiers, because their reputation was well known. The refugees had heard of the atrocities members of the Red Army had committed against Germans in areas under Soviet occupation. The many acts of cruelty were made known, not only through official news and propaganda, but also through numerous rumors that made the rounds.

To make matters worse, in spite of having planned official evacuations, the authorities of the Third Reich delayed acting on them until it was too late. By then they were overwhelmed by the sheer number of people who wanted to flee. This, and the panic caused by the speed of the Russian advance, as well as the many refugees killed in the crossfire, and finally the inclement winter weather, resulted in the deaths of thousands of people.

Most Germans who were not evacuated from East Prussia and other German territories east of the Oder-Neisse line during the war were expelled after World War II had ended and, instead of being called *Flüchtlinge* (refugees) they were known as *Heimatvertriebene* (expellees).

With the German attack on the Soviet Union repulsed and Soviet troops entering Germany and Hungary in 1944, the number of rapes reached a level

Sirens

of, until then, unknown proportions. Little is known for certain today about what happened in the path of the Red Army as they re-conquered former Soviet territory such as the Ukraine and the Balkan states, but countless men of those countries joined the *Waffen SS* (*Waffen Schutzstaffel* or Weapons Defense Detachment) to defend their homeland, and their women against the Soviets when soldiers of the Red Army approached.

And while the Nazi atrocities in Poland ended in late 1944, Soviet oppression continued.

After about two million Soviet soldiers died in captivity, the remainder of the Red Army took unspeakable reprisals on the German population. Some German soldiers, after retaking a small town in East Prussia from the Russians, found indescribable horrors. The few villagers who survived, all old men, women and children since the men had gone to war, had gruesome stories to tell about Russian atrocities. Subsequently, people fled East Prussia en masse.

The Christmas of 1944 was the last many families spent in their ancestral homeland in the East. Every weekend civilians, POWs and German troops dug defense trenches around villages and the outskirts of larger towns; and the stream of refugees became a flood.

The church bells of some towns rang continuously as a warning to abandon homes and flee toward the West. The Russians soon reached the outlying farms and villages – the bringers of death were at the gate.

Despite the very difficult decision, many families left immediately, taking with them only what they could carry. Towns were in chaos, with huge crowds of civilians as well as wounded soldiers trying to get on trains to escape from the Russian nightmare. At the same time, the Allied bombers and fighter planes had total control of the skies. They shot civilians and also sank ships that were loaded with refugees who were attempting to flee from the soldiers of the Red Army.

Death was all around. Many people committed suicide rather than face the Russians. Others went so far as to poison their children to keep the Russians from capturing them alive.

More than two million people died in the eastern provinces of Germany toward the end of the war while fleeing from the advancing Red Army, some of them froze or staved to death, but the main death toll occurred when the refugees were caught up by the Russian soldiers. They were run over by tanks, robbed or shot, while the women and young girls were raped and then left to die.

It has been estimated that by the end of World War II Red Army soldiers had raped more than two million German women and young girls, children really, with an estimated 200,000 dying from injuries sustained during the rapes, from committing suicide after the rapes, or by being murdered outright.

*   *   *

Many of the refugees were transported by freight trains and came from Silesia, Hungary and Czechoslovakia. One of these trains, packed with refugees, went from the city of Karlsruhe to Pforzheim. Along the route, at each station, a car was uncoupled and left there while the passengers of that car, along with their luggage which often weighed less than 150 pounds and contained all of their possessions, were handed over to the authorities of the town. This was in an area of Germany that had not been touched much by the war and few buildings and houses had been hit by bombs, and now the town's citizens were ordered to share their homes with those less fortunate, who were able to tell them horrible stories about the Russians. However, numerous refugees still found no home and had to live in camps for a number of years.

Sirens

*   *   *

Even before the war ended, when the Red Army was advancing, large numbers of refugees from all over the eastern areas of the German Reich including *Ostpreußen*, *Pommern* and *Schlesien*, fled toward the West. By January 1945, fleeing from the advancing Soviet forces, the German refugees trudged through snow at temperatures of minus 25 degrees Celsius (minus 13 degrees Fahrenheit) while Soviet aircraft shot at them. Many of the refugees died during this exodus.

Also in January 1945, late in the month, the 3rd Belarusian Front surrounded the city of Königsberg on the landward side, cutting off the route to the port city of Pillau and trapping a German panzer troop, as well as 200,000 civilians, in the city. The civilians had three choices: Stay in the city and starve, which was easy to do when the ration consisted of only 180 grams of bread per day; cross the front lines and throw themselves on the mercies of the Soviets who were not likely to show pity; or cross the frozen waters of the lagoon to Pillau in hopes of finding a place on one of the evacuation ships. Hundreds chose to cross the front line, but about 2,000 women and children crossed the ice to Pillau on foot every day.

The final Soviet assault on Königsberg began on April 12, with heavy bombardment of the town. Those civilian who had chosen to remain in the city died by the thousands.

One family fleeing toward the West linked up with part of the retreating German army. The husband pleaded with the soldiers to take them along, but many of the vehicles passed them by before one of the trucks stopped. The family was eventually allowed to ride on the truck, simply because they had four girls and because of what the Russians might do to those girls.

Germans from all over the east had quickly learned what these brutal, bloodthirsty Russian soldiers

Ursula (Winter) Turner

were capable of inflicting on innocent victims. The soldiers advanced unchecked from the east toward the west at the end of the war, with millions of desperate refugees preceding them, clogging roads and seeking shelter from the dreadfully cold winter in empty houses and barns.

The rampage of the Red Army went on during the occupation of the rest of eastern Germany and often led to occurrences such as happened in the small town of Demmin which had been conquered by Soviet forces in the spring of 1945. It was an unconditional and complete surrender, without prior fighting in or around the town. Nearly 900 people committed suicide after the town was declared open for looting and pillaging to the soldiers by Soviet commanders.

In the end it did work out to some extent for many of those who survived this ordeal because, without the workers and professional experience of the refugees, the rebuilding of Germany, which began in 1948, would have taken much longer. And often, the original citizens as well as those who had come from the East, ended up living in better conditions than they had before the Second World War.

*   *   *

Heinz Walter, who later became my sister's husband, and his mother, were among those fleeing toward the west from Ostpreußen. His sister, Erna, and her small family had already been evacuated from their home on October 19, 1944 and had been sent to the city of Frankenberg in the state of *Sachsen* (Saxony). Heinz, 14 years old at the time, and his mother left their home in a small town near Tilsit either at the end of November or the beginning of December. They decided to leave because the Russians were approaching at a fast pace and coming ever closer. They left their hometown with a horse drawn wagon, loaded with as many belongings as they'd been able to pile on it. They attempted to spend their nights at farm houses because of the freezing weather, but they were always turned away. Somewhere along their route they managed to catch a train. They were also able to briefly visit Erna in Frankenberg.

Both Heinz and his mother have since died and a lot of the details of their flight from the Russians are no longer known, but Erna thinks they went across an ice-covered lake and joined other refugees who were heading toward the Baltic Sea. They arrived at a city there, possibly Königsberg, which was full of soldiers and other refugees, all waiting for an opportunity to get away. The Russians had surrounded the city and the only way out of Ostpreußen was by water.

"One ship became famous," said Mechthild. "The 'Wilhelm Gustloff' was fully loaded with refugees when it lifted anchor and set out across the water for the West." Most ships were shot at and bombs were dropped as well. "But the 'Gustloff' made it with Heinz and his mother on it," said my sister, "although poor Heinz had a few rough moments when his mother refused to get on the narrow plank that connected the land to the ship. At last, in desperation, he asked for help and some of the other refugees assisted him in getting his mother on board."

After they disembarked on the western shore of the Baltic Sea, the Gustloff returned to pick up more refugees. Once more fully loaded, the ship was attacked again. This time it was hit and sank with all on board.

Of course, some people did not flee from the eastern part of Germany but chose to remain there, although few realized what they would be facing after the war ended.

Ursula (Winter) Turner

My brother-in-law, Heinz Walter

*   *   *

Hannelore Wittenbecher, who still lives in the former East Germany, was given special permission to visit my family when she was about 12. This would be her only trip to the west until the country became one again. She has some gruesome stories to tell, stories she mostly heard from her mother-in-law and her parents.

Sirens

Mrs. Wittenbecher, Hannelore's mother-in-law, lived in the city of Nauen and spent the time from January to April 1945 in the hospital with a severe case of pleurisy which she had most likely contracted while sitting in her damp cellar during the many bombing attacks on the city. During her stay, all the window panes of the hospital were broken four times due to vibrations from bombs being dropped nearby. After the last attack on April 20, Hitler's birthday, the hospital was evacuated and the sick woman was discharged, weighing only 90 pounds. At the beginning of May of that same year, the entire city of Nauen was evacuated at which time Mrs. Wittenbecher and all of her family became refugees. However, the road they needed to take was filled with people who were also fleeing, as well as with German army units who were trying to get to the West, and it took the Wittenbechers, father, mother and small son, an hour to get into line on this road. They had brought one small and one large hand-pulled wagon and a baby buggy, all loaded down with their possessions.

The Wittenbechers had planned to stop at a small town about 20 kilometers (12 miles) away where they had relatives, but when they got to the side road that led to this town, they had to let the handicapped people go first. By this time Mrs. Wittenbecher was at the end of her strength. Other refugees promised to notify the relatives who quickly came with bicycles to help them make it to their house, where they were able to stay for about a week. At this time they decided to return home taking back roads to avoid the main highway.

However, in the meantime the Red Army had arrived in Nauen, which was the county seat. The Russians had taken over the courthouse, and Mrs. Wittenbecher was made to do the cleaning for them. But when the Russian officers' wives discovered that she was a good seamstress, she was instead ordered to sew their dresses and they gave her food in return.

Hannelore's father was drafted in 1933 and fought in Poland, France and Russia. He was severely wounded while fighting near Moscow and was flown from there to an infirmary in Tübingen. But when he heard that the English would be occupying that town the next day, he and others fled during the night and walked home to Erfurt where the Americans had already arrived. However, the state of Thüringen, where Erfurt was located, was exchanged with the Russians on August 2, 1945, for West Berlin, and therefore Hannelore Wittenbecher's family (she hadn't been born yet) ended up in the Soviet Zone, which became East Germany.

Sirens

Chapter 10
The War is Over

One morning, when I was almost four and a half years old (May 8, 1945), we heard shouts and laughter coming through our open windows, something not heard in our streets for a very long time, and never by me. I was still sleepy and didn't pay much attention to what was happening, but soon Mutti came into our room, doing a little shouting of her own. "The war is over. The war is finally over!" she cried. There was, along with the tears streaming from her eyes, the biggest grin on her face I had ever seen.

Mechthild jumped out of bed and the two of them hugged each other and danced around the room. Although I didn't know what it all meant, I, too, jumped out of bed and joined my mother and sister in their dance.

With the radio rarely working and few papers being printed, especially in our rural area, I don't know how word spread so quickly. Mutti supposed that most of the women down in the street had heard it from the town crier who still made his rounds every day, stopping at selected street corners, ringing his bell and shouting what was usually local news at the top of his lungs. However, what Mutti now heard from the women on the street as she stuck her head out the window, was not local news – it was world news. The war was, indeed, over – at least for the people of Germany.

Although my mother and sister were very excited about this news, and although I laughed and carried on with them, I really didn't understand what all the excitement was about. It meant nothing to me. I couldn't figure out why people were getting so wound up about this news. I was unacquainted with peacetime life and couldn't see where anything had changed – at

Ursula (Winter) Turner

least not just then. However, the women, who made up the majority of the adult population of our town at that time, as well as the older children, who could remember a time without war, could hardly wait for things to go back to "normal."

But going back to normal was not something that happened overnight. It took a very long time for the German people to get back to their former way of life – and many never could. Those who'd had to flee from their homes in the East and those who'd lost their houses to the bombs would never be able to return to what they called home. And many, many women had lost their husbands and had to try and make new lives for themselves.

One major, immediate change was the silence. Even I noticed that. The sound of the air-raid sirens was a thing of the past, as was the noise of the planes that used to drop the bombs from the sky and sent people for cover or to their death. Otherwise our lives changed little after we first heard the glad tidings.

Several days after the unofficial news had hit the streets, it was confirmed. Mechthild, then almost 15, who could still remember a time without bombs, a time with plenty of food and a time when our father, whom I didn't know at all, was still at home, teaching in a classroom below us, happened to be looking out of the living room window one day. She thought she saw movement against the backdrop of the hill on the other side of the valley. Something or someone was moving along the road. She quickly discovered that these were the first of the American soldiers who were about to enter Allendorf. However, she was somewhat puzzled by their appearance. Mechthild had never seen Negroes, and these soldiers were black. What scared her was that, from this distance, she was unable to see any of their faces against the dark background of the hill. She rushed into the kitchen which faced in the opposite direction to warn Mutti who was busy fixing lunch while I watched her from my usual position on the footstool, and she shouted excitedly, "Mutti, Mutti, come quick. The American soldiers are coming and they have no heads!"

Mutti was naturally skeptical, about what Mechthild was telling her, but wanted to see for herself what would have made her older, usually level-headed daughter, say something so ridiculous. She wiped her hands on a corner of her apron and followed Mechthild to the living room.

There was nothing to be seen. By then the soldiers had advanced toward the first of the houses and were hidden from our view. Mutti returned to her dinner preparations and chalked Mechthild's observation up to the excitement of seeing her first Americans. "Soldiers without heads, indeed," she muttered.

Mechthild insisted. "I know they were American soldiers because they were wearing olive green colored uniforms, not gray ones. I just couldn't see any faces."

In the meantime Mutti was trying to come up with a reason why these soldiers would come to our small community, if they were indeed Americans. But she was glad they had arrived because it was the final confirmation for us that the war was truly over.

They were a cautious bunch, this advance group of the American Forces. Not having met any resistance so far, they nevertheless crept around the corner of our street, guns held at the ready, apparently expecting an attack at any moment. They got a pleasant surprise. None of the women, children and old men was interested in harming these men; on the contrary, they were all happy to see them, because it proved to them that peace had, at last, come to our war-torn country. No longer would anyone have to flee to the basement at the sound of sirens. In fact, the sirens had been stopped forever, or so everybody hoped. The men of the village would surely return soon, too, and people could live in peace and normalcy once again.

Several of the soldiers nevertheless, stopped at the corner house and entered it to check it out. They found only two middle aged women and their mother on the premises. Others proceeded on toward the school which was the next building, separated from the corner house by a large garden and the entranceway to the school yard.

The main door of our building was never kept locked during the day. The entrance to the classrooms was at the opposite side of the building, although we could get there from our side through a regular inside door at the bottom of the stairway.

Two of the American soldiers clomped up the first set of stairs with their heavy army boots. Frau Schol, who was just coming down from the upper floor with a basket of laundry, squeezed herself against the wall to let them pass, then stared after them because she had never encountered Negroes either. The men stopped at our apartment door and rang the bell.

When Mutti opened the door, assuming it was a neighbor, anxious to tell her the news about the soldiers having arrived in town (she'd not expected that the "enemy" soldiers would bother with doorbells but had thought it more likely that they would smash in the door), this 5-foot, 1-inch woman found herself face to face with two large, black American G.I.s. She was stunned since she, too, was unfamiliar with black people and, until this encounter, had seen them only in pictures. There were few Negroes living in Germany at that time, and none in our area.

The Americans had a message for Mutti. I don't know how my mother and these soldiers communicated. Perhaps the Americans spoke German; I know Mutti knew just a few words of English she'd learned in secretarial school. Regardless, she was somehow informed that, since the school was public property, the part of the American Army that would be occupying our area planned to make the building their headquarters. I learned later that other families were made to leave their privately owned homes as well to be taken over by soldiers. Elsa's family was one of them. At any rate we, along with all the other tenants of the school, had exactly two hours to get ourselves out, along with whatever we could manage to take with us.

Mutti, used to hardships by now, knew it would be useless to complain or resist. In fact doing so, might actually cause more problems for us. But what could she, two kids, and our grandmother pack up and carry in two hours' time? And where were we supposed to take our belongings? Removing any kind of furniture was out of the question, except for perhaps a few very small pieces. We packed up clothing and some bedding into suitcases, put a few dishes in a box and took whatever else we could carry out to the front yard for the time being until Mutti and Oma could figure out where to go from there.

Although the other tenants had to move out as well, they all had relatives in town with whom they could find temporary shelter until other arrangements could be made or until they could move back home.

At last the four of us were the only ones left, sitting on our suitcases in front of the school, with Mutti and Lenchen Oma still trying to decide where we might go. Oma wasn't really any help since she was only a visitor to town and knew few of the people.

Then, before they could come up with an answer, it presented itself in the form of a neighbor lady who lived a couple of houses away from the school. She came toward us, hesitant at first, as though she wasn't sure how to approach us or whether she should say anything at all. But then she touched Mutti's shoulder and spoke up, "Frau Winter," she said, "I'm so sorry about what has happened to you and your family. I'd like to invite you to stay with us, but I can only offer you a space in the basement. The house is full of relatives from the city who came to us looking for a place to stay after their homes were destroyed by bombs. But at least you'll be indoors and dry, and it's not so cold right now, so the basement should be livable." She looked embarrassed about the fact that the cellar was all she could offer us. Mutti was so glad to have been offered a place for us to stay that she gratefully accepted.

She had packed her good dishes into the larger of the wicker clothes baskets, and, after covering them with a towel, she and Oma had carried them to our basement before we left, hoping they would be safe there. Everything else we had to leave behind while the neighbor lady, Frau Krumm, and some of her relatives helped us carry the things we'd been able to bring to our front yard to her house.

*   *   *

The Würtz family was to live in that house later on. Their daughter, Elisabeth, another friend of mine just a month older than I, has her own memories of the war and its aftermath. She and her family were living in her grandmother's house at that time, just a few houses up the hill from us. They too listened for the sirens and rushed to the basement on a regular basis when they started up with their wailing.

"My mother would wake me up and have me put on some clothes while she carried Oma, who could not walk, down the stairs," she said. Elisabeth remembers sitting on chairs on either side of the stairs for some reason she did not understand, since it was a large basement and had many rooms. Her uncle, who was a shoemaker, had his shop in one of the rooms which had an outside entrance. There was old furniture stored everywhere. There was also a room that contained the standard copper kettle in which to do the laundry.

Sirens

Elisabeth remembers one time when the sirens went off and she was outside. She hid under the gooseberry bush because she didn't want to come in and once again go to the dark basement. "My mother was getting upset and when she finally found me, I got it good," she said

However, the worst air strike Elisabeth remembers happened when they were away from home. "We were at the bakery when the sirens started up," she said, "and everybody went to the basement under the store. When we got the all-clear and came back up, we saw that the town of Haiger was burning. It was a terrible fire and a lot of people died that day because there were a lot of visitors who had come to the funeral of people who had been bombed a couple of days earlier." Many people can tell tales of seeing entire cities burning after a night-time bombing attack.

"When the Americans came with their big trucks, they drove them everywhere," Elisabeth remembers. "They drove them over fences and all over Oma's garden," she said. "They flattened it without regard for anything. I remember getting upset about it. I loved my Oma very much and they destroyed her garden."

However, other than the destruction of the garden, the G.I.s did not bother the Würtz family, although they did make them move from their living quarters in the house to the basement, while the soldiers took over the upstairs. "Oma had a big house," said Elisabeth," two floors and an attic besides the basement." Some cousins came to live with them and had to sleep in the potato bins on top of the potatoes. "Mother said we were lucky they (the Americans) did not make us leave the house. She thought this might have been because her grandmother was sick."

One of the soldiers always parked his jeep right by the back door. Since it was springtime, Elisabeth had gone into the garden to pick a handful of violets. "He was standing next to his jeep when I got back," she recalls, "and he wanted to trade me the violets for a Hershey chocolate bar. I did not want to do that because there were too many of us to share the chocolate with. In the end I walked away with the entire box of Hershey bars."

*   *   *

Many of the items we had not been able to take with us when we were forced to leave our apartment we found later in the schoolyard and under the kitchen windows where the American soldiers had thrown them, claiming they had been in their way. "We went through these things," Mechthild reminded me later, "and saved what was usable and not broken."

Elsa and her family had to live with nearby relatives, but they were allowed back into their home after only two or three weeks. Our exile lasted much longer. Their house was built in such a way that the stable where the cows were kept was directly under the living room. Elsa told me that the floor of that room was always warm. There was no barn. Elsa's father, who was one of the first men to return to the village from the front, got permission to come to his home every morning and evening during the time they didn't live there, to milk their two cows.

Initially we had been glad to have been offered the basement accommodations by the neighbor lady, but her basement was really more of a cellar. It was unfinished and was used to store potatoes, turnips and apples from the Krumm's apple orchard.

During the day we spent our time with the others upstairs, but at night we had to sleep on the meager pile of potatoes because it was the slightest bit warmer there then on the cold, bare floor, although quite lumpy. It was spring, but May nights are still quite cold in Germany and the cellar was damp and very dark. For light we had a lamp that used carbide for fuel the odor of which made me sick to my stomach to the point of causing me to vomit. I don't encounter that odor often these days, but I still feel nauseous when I get even as much as a small whiff of the stuff.

I still remember the unpleasantness of it all and recall thinking at the time: "If this is what peace is like, I want the war back!"

When we were offered a room by a family friend who lived halfway up the hill and in the center of the village, I was very happy when Mutti accepted it. We lived there until we were able to return to our apartment a couple of months later. Until that time, we left most of our things in the barn of the Krumm's home where we had originally stored them.

*   *   *

During the time we were gone from our apartment, I met my first Americans up close and personal. When still living in the basement of the house that was located close to the school building, I often went outside to play with the other children from the neighborhood, including Elsa and, sometimes, Elisabeth. With our benefactor's house so full of people, she was probably glad to get me out from underfoot once in a while. It was May, the weather was nice, and I certainly needed the fresh air after the ordeal of spending my nights in the musty, smelly cellar.

It was not surprising that we children were drawn to the school building. We wanted to get a closer look at the foreign soldiers, who now lived there, at those Americans who had taken over the school and all of the apartments. They might have been our enemy in the past, but it was quite evident that they loved kids. I never learned any of their names, or if I did, they were so foreign sounding to me at the time that I can't remember them now. One man, however, left a deep impression that has stayed in my mind to this day. I can still see him as though he were standing in front of me. At the time he seemed old, but he was probably only in his mid twenties. He had red hair, cut short in the military style, and a ruddy complexion with small scars all over his face, most likely from acne, and he had lots and lots of freckles. I can remember most clearly that the first joint of one of his index fingers was missing. I chose him, from all the others, to become my father figure.

This soldier often carried me around piggy-back on his shoulders. He gave me my first taste of chocolate, and chocolate, or any candy, is heaven to kids. The gum he gave me was promptly swallowed as soon as the taste was gone. He finally got it through to me that you don't swallow gum. For an extra special treat he once invited me, along with the other children, to my family's former kitchen where he and his buddies entertained us with a puppet show, using their socks for the puppets and standing behind the door to the pantry. Although we didn't understand a word they said, we all, including the soldiers, I'm sure, had a wonderful time.

These men, who surely suffered their share of hardships during a long and difficult war far away from home, thought nothing of being kind to the children of their former enemy – children who didn't have any idea what the war had been about, who had never known any other kind of life, and who were excited to be getting a little attention from these men. None of us had been around any men except for the very old ones of our village. Although toward the end of the war the school had not been open for lessons for about a year while the classrooms had been occupied by German soldiers, malnourished, sick or wounded, we'd been told to stay away from them because they were dirty and covered with lice. None of us knew our fathers. And the Americans showed us a good time with what was available to them, and they made a few children very happy.

Sirens

Today I truly wish I knew the name of these kind men, particularly the one who used to carry me around and showed me special attention. Perhaps some of them are still alive and think back to their time they spent in Germany and remember the small children they entertained. I would love to be able to thank them. Only after I grew to adulthood was I able to realize what those men did for all of us.

* * *

In my parents' hometown, Launsbach, the Americans arrived before war's end, around the middle of March.

"We could see, on the day before they came to us, the American tanks as they drove past our train station while heading for Wißmar (a neighboring town)," said my cousin, Dieter. "In Wißmar they were stopped, because some fanatical young German soldier shot at them with an anti-tank gun," Dieter continued. "The tanks pulled back and fired into the village, killing several civilians."

On the same day the German soldiers from the *Waffen SS* left Launsbach, and people showed white fabric at their windows. A little while later somebody shouted, "The SS is coming back!" The white cloths immediately disappeared from the windows.

"The *Waffen SS* was an elite army unit which had, until that time, been stationed in Launsbach for quite a while," said Dieter. "If people had been caught by them as they were waving a white flag, they might have been shot."

The Americans came to Launsbach the next evening after dark and undertook a house to house search. "Later some came back," said Dieter, "and we had to move from our second-story apartment in with our first-floor tenants which made living conditions quite crowded." The tenants had several children, and there was Tante Gertrud with her three boys. Lenchen Oma was visiting with us at that time.

"The Americans made themselves comfortable upstairs," said Dieter, "and even drove one of their tanks into our yard. By the way," he continued, "that was the first time I saw a Negro."

Later on some Germans collected Nazi memorabilia such as uniforms, belts, pistols and helmets or caps. They were a hot item on the black market because the Americans wanted them as souvenirs and would trade them for sugar, flour, coffee and, naturally, cigarettes.

Sirens

Chapter 11
The Russians Enter Berlin

While my small family did face some additional tough times even though the war had ended, including having to leave our home and having to live in a dank basement, although only temporarily, and losing many of our belongings, we felt lucky to be living in the American sector of Germany. The American soldiers treated us in a fairly decent manner, being especially nice to the smaller children.

People in other parts of the country faced much greater hardships. Numerous Germans, especially the women who lived in the Russian sector suffered many cruelties at the hands of the Russian soldiers after the war was over.

One of my German friends, Karin Hamilton, who also lives in America now having married an American soldier, was born in Berlin only a couple of months after the war had ended.

Karin's family had originally lived in Westpreußen (West Prussia). One night, toward the end of the war, when Karin's mother was already pregnant with her, the SS awakened her father in the middle of the night. They pointed a gun at him and told him to "serve or die." They did not permit him to get dressed, but yanked him from his bed and took him away. He served in Russia and Italy and later became a prisoner of war of the British and was held on the island of Malta. He returned home when Karin was two years old.

Her mother and two sisters, then fourteen and twelve, were forced to flee from their home because the Russians were closing in on them. They, too, had heard of the atrocities these soldiers were capable of and decided not to take any chances. They managed to get on a train to Berlin where Karin's Tante Maria owned a butcher shop. The girls had to smear ashes on their faces, wear scarves, and walk as though they were crippled to keep from being raped by the Russian soldiers, especially after these soldiers occupied Berlin. They had to put up with Russians even though they lived in the American sector.

Karin (Tetschlag) Hamilton at age 2, about the time when she first met her father.

Living in the Russian Zone was so much more dangerous for the German population than living in the American Zone, where I grew up, or the British or

Sirens

French Zones which made up the rest of Germany after the war.

When the Russians came to Berlin, their territory ended less than half a kilometer (about ¼ mile) from the butcher shop in West Berlin where Karin's family now lived and where she was born on July 5, 1945. However, this did not stop the Russian soldiers from visiting this area at will. The S-Bahn (Schnellbahn or speed train) bridge was the border between East and West. The Russians crossed this border and got drunk, and then they plundered the homes and businesses of the civilian population and raped the women, no matter what their age.

"My aunt and my mother were fortunate to have some wine and brandy and a little meat to offer these soldiers," said Karin. "It kept them from being raped. But the Russians did take their jewelry. I can't tell you how many times I heard my aunt say how glad she was they had something to give to those Russians so all they did was steal from them instead of raping them," she added.

Back then all watches had to be wound to keep them running. When any watch the Russians had stolen stopped ticking and no longer told the correct time, they shot the person they had stolen it from because they felt they'd been cheated by them. They didn't know enough to wind the watches. These soldiers also didn't know what a flush toilet was. Consequently they washed themselves as well as food, such as potatoes, in the water of the toilet bowl. If anything was accidentally flushed away, the home owners were beaten or shot.

"Next to the butcher shop stood a shoe store," said Karin. "The Soviets stole shoes for themselves and burned their worn-out boots on the sidewalk in front of the building."

By the time Karin's father came home, his family had moved to an apartment about a block from the butcher shop and a little farther away from the Russian occupied zone. The West German Mark stood at about one to four against the East German Mark. Karin remembers that, when she was a little older, she sometimes was given 10 Pfennig by her mother to spend on herself, which she exchanged for 40 East German Pfennig. Then she went across the border into the Russian sector and bought chicken broth for 30 Pfennig. "It was so good," she said.

West Berlin (light color) surrounded by East Germany

    Postwar Germany had been divided into four sectors. The allied part was controlled by the United States, Britain and France, while the remainder was under Soviet rule. The city of Berlin, located inside the Soviet sector, was also divided into four sections. In June 1948, the Soviets made an attempt to control all of Berlin. The method they used to try and accomplish this was to not allow anyone to cross any part of East Germany, thereby starving the population of West Berlin and cutting off their businesses. The Truman administration reacted by implementing a continual airlift, with planes flying day and night, dropping much-needed supplies into the city of West Berlin.

    Karin remembers and was also told by family members that they received such items as sugar, dried milk, flour, noodles, rice, candy and gum, canned meat, soup and toothpaste through this airlift. She remembers the candy and gum best. This Luftbrücke (Air Bridge) to Berlin lasted until September 1949, although on May 12 of that year the Soviet government yielded and lifted the blockade.

"My uncle, Tante Maria's husband who had come back from the war to take over his butcher shop again, got rich by taking jewelry for payment in return for giving people more meat than they were allowed on their ration cards," said Karin. "The East Germans usually got a list of what they were permitted to buy, such as potatoes, bread, sugar, salt, and so on. Then they had to stand in line for hours to buy these items, and many of them often came away empty-handed because everything was sold out by the time it came to their turn. And when these things were gone, they were gone!" Except for the fact that they no longer had to worry about bombs, their way of life had not changed much after the war was over.

When she was about five or six years old, Karin remembers her family sometimes traded on the black market. They would take items across the border to the East, such as coffee and butter and return with cigarettes or candy. The contraband was carried across the border by Karin, who always wore a big, long dress with pockets sewn on the inside. Children were not searched by the young Russian soldiers who manned the border crossings. They were more interested in begging for cigarettes for themselves.

Karin's family often assisted other refugees who had escaped from the East much later than they had and had nobody in Berlin who could help them. These people usually ended up in a Flüchtlingslager (refugee camp). "My God, I don't think I will ever forget the sights and sounds and stench of that place," said Karin. "There stood cot after cot after cot, with sheets in between. Babies were screaming. Men and women were crying. They had nothing but the clothes on their back. It was gruesome."

Ursula (Winter) Turner

She remembers visiting two couples from the camp later on. One had moved to an apartment house at the outskirts of Berlin; the other lived, along with their two small children, in a little place – three rooms and an outhouse – with a small garden.

Karin has never gotten over the impression of the day when the Berlin Wall went up. "It was on a Sunday morning", she recalls. "Since it was my job to get the Sunday paper from the kiosk at the corner opposite from my aunt's butcher shop, I was the first in my family to see it happen." It was about 8 or 8:30 a.m. on August 13, 1961. Karin was 16 at the time. "I came down our street and heard this strange rumble," she remembers. "As I turned the corner toward the train bridge, I saw an American tank in the middle of the street, facing the bridge. It was flanked by a French and a British tank sitting on side streets. Their guns were all pointed toward the border.

Karin had to go past the Americans and toward the French tank to get her paper. As she came closer, she saw Russian soldiers building a wall along the border. Behind them, facing toward the West, stood Soviet tanks with their guns trained at the Allied tanks but, at the same time also at their own comrades.

"I ran to my aunt's house after I saw this and told them there was another war starting, then I came home and told my parents the same thing," said Karin. Soon everyone in the neighborhood was on the street, swearing at the Soviets and telling them to leave the border alone. The allied soldiers in their tanks stood by with their weapons ready – never saying a word – just watching.

This was a black day for Berlin citizens because the Wall separated them from family members whom they didn't see for years afterward. Others lost property on the other side of the Wall from them, both East and West.

People on the west side of the Berlin Wall would build platforms to stand on to see if they could spot a relative or friend on the other side.

It had been Soviet Premier Nikita Krushev's wish to have this wall erected so that "no wolf can break it down," with which he meant the allies. The Germans called the Wall *Schandmauer* (wall of shame). It eventually stretched for 155 kilometers (96 miles) all around the city of West Berlin.

Some 3,000 East Germans fled to the West in just 24 hours before the borders were closed.

When President John F. Kennedy came to Berlin and made his famous statement: *"Ich bin ein Berliner,"* on June 26, 1963, Karin was 18 and going to trade school. Her class attended the event and Karin heard JFK speak.

Ursula (Winter) Turner

Chapter 12
Moving Back Home

The Americans eventually decided that, with no big cities nearby, our area wasn't important enough to have a headquarters located there, and the soldiers moved out of whatever homes they had taken over and occupied and moved on to different parts of the country. I missed my new friend a great deal. However, this meant we could move back home. After Mutti thanked our hostess profusely for her hospitality, we did just that. But we weren't prepared for what awaited us.

Mutti almost went into shock after we entered our apartment. The place, which she had always struggled so hard to keep clean and neat and organized, in spite of her limited time and resources, was a shambles. The floor was dirty, and littered with bits of paper and cigarette butts. Cabinet doors and drawers stood wide open with many of the contents we had not been able to take with us strewn on the floor as well. A lot of the dishes were broken, in the cupboard as well as on the floor. A number of the towels that we'd left behind were oily and greasy. They'd apparently been used to clean guns. Papa's beautiful, old oak desk had heel marks and cigarette burns marring its surface.

After a few days Mutti determined that many of our possessions were missing. We never found them again. They were probably among the items that had been thrown out of the windows, and dishonest neighbors had found them and claimed them as their own. During the war a lot of citizens looked out for themselves first and worried about others later, with a few exceptions such as the ladies who had taken us in when we had nowhere else to go

Our radio was gone. Although we hadn't been able to receive much on it toward the end of the war, news coverage had been picking up again and Mutti so wanted to listen to the radio in hopes of catching any bits of information that was given about how soon the German soldiers might be expected to return home. The ones who had been quartered in the classrooms below us were no longer there and were, presumably, on their way home.

When any soldiers from Allendorf came home, Mutti always paid them a visit and asked if they had run into Papa anywhere. None ever had. Of the daily letters she had sent him, twenty-seven had been returned to her, and Papa was officially declared missing in action. Some time later, Mutti was informed that he was a prisoner of war of the Americans and was being held somewhere in France. Now Mutti kept hoping nothing would happen to him there, especially since the war was over, and that he'd be released soon. She expected him to appear on our doorstep at any moment. She and Mechthild missed him a great deal. To me he was just a stranger. As far as I knew, I had never met him, although he had come home once when I was only a baby which, of course, I didn't remember. Consequently, I had no reason to miss him. Besides, I liked our set-up just fine the way it was, with Mutti and Mechthild as my family, and with Oma as an occasional visitor.

Mutti's biggest shock after returning to our home came when she went to the basement to get her good dishes. The basket was still in place and the dishes were in it, but every single one of them had been smashed beyond repair. It looked as though somebody had deliberately stomped around in the basket while wearing heavy boots such as soldiers wore, until not one single dish could be salvaged. Mutti and Papa had received this set of dishes for their wedding and Mutti had treasured it. I had gone to the basement with her and, when she discovered her loss I saw her slowly sit down on a wooden crate and, although she was trying to hide it from me by burying her face in her hands, she began to cry. That was one of the few times I had ever seen her cry throughout all those horrible years of the war. Breaking her dishes was such a senseless act of cruelty that she simply could not absorb it, and to her it was the final blow on top of what she'd found upstairs.

Oma was still with us at the time. With few trains running and the ones that did loaded with exhausted soldiers returning home from the front, she had not yet been able to go back to her home. She filled her time by helping Mutti reestablish order in our apartment. In the process of her work, she discovered, way back in the lower part of the kitchen cupboard, some strange items that turned out to be the disassembled parts of a radio. At first the women didn't know what to do with them and were ready to throw them away. Then Mutti remembered an old man who lived at the other end of the village and who used to repair radios in his spare time. She took the parts, and the housing, which she'd found in the pantry, to him with the slight hope that he might be able to assemble them so we'd have a working radio again. After tinkering with the parts for a few days and replacing some missing ones with some he had on hand, he was actually able to put everything together again. When Mutti picked up her new radio, she paid him with a jar of honey and he was happy with his pay. He'd been bored anyway and had needed something to do. There was one problem with this gadget however. After it had warmed up and had played for a while, it would suddenly decide to quit. This was quite frustrating because the announcer might be in the middle of a news story Mutti had been listening to and he would be cut off in mid-sentence. But my mother soon discovered that, if you gave the top of the radio a whack with your fist, it would start playing again. After a while I became the designated whacker. If Mutti was busy with cooking or another chore while listening to a program, and the radio decided to quit, she would say, "Ursula, smack the radio, but not too hard." She never did learn anything about Papa from it, but it was a nice distraction from her worries and from her heavy daily workload. Later, after Papa had already been home for a while and the radio kept quitting more and more often, my parents finally broke down and bought a new one. This was two or three years after the war had ended and some things were once again available for purchase in the stores.

During the general cleanup of our apartment, Oma found something else in our kitchen cupboard that piqued her interest. It was a metal object that had a slight resemblance to a pineapple and featured a small ring at the top. Since German hand grenades look somewhat like an old fashioned potato masher and not at all like this object, Oma had no idea that the thing she was holding in her hand was the American version. She wandered all over the house, ringing doorbells, and asking everybody she met if they knew what the object was. At last an old man who was there to visit the Löbers came to the rescue and, carefully taking the hand grenade from Lenchen Oma's hand, explained to her what it was. They were somewhere on the stairs at the time and Oma had to quickly lower herself onto one of the steps because her legs had become slightly weak when she heard the news. I don't know for certain what the old gentleman did with the grenade but I did hear a loud bang not too long after this incident and Mutti told me that she thought the man had gone to the bottom of the schoolyard and had thrown the grenade into the field.

One day Oma's head started itching something awful. "You have head lice," Mutti told her after inspecting her hair carefully. "You probably got them as a souvenir from the soldiers who were staying in the classrooms." Oma had been down there cleaning up some of the mess that had been left behind when they had been moved out.

After Mutti's pronouncement, another item found in the cupboard, left behind by the Americans, did come in handy. Mutti knew enough English to figure out what the label on the can said. Besides, the words were very similar in both languages. She read "Insect Powder," which would have translated into German as *Insekten Pulver*. She sprinkled it liberally on Oma's gray head. The poor woman then covered it tightly with a headscarf. The resulting itching caused by the insects as they were trying to escape must have been almost unbearable and just about drove my grandmother insane. But the powder did its job and got rid of the lice without any of the rest of us suffering from them.

After Oma had finished cleaning the classrooms, we all helped her carry bags and boxes of the trash that had been left behind by the German as well as the American soldiers into the center of the school yard to be burned. For a long time, while the fire burned, and later smoldered, nobody could go to that side of the building because, although nobody had realized it, there had been live ammunition among the things we'd carried out to the pile of trash, and this kept going off, making it dangerous to be in the vicinity of the fire.

We also found some canned goods, rations of sorts, that the American G.I.s hadn't bothered to take away with them. Mutti placed these in the pantry, and they certainly helped us out with our meager supplies since we still couldn't buy much at the grocery or any of the other stores. And we still had to use our ration cards for everything we wanted to purchase, a different colored card for each item: Fat, meat, milk, sugar, even shoes, everything we needed in our daily lives. Each card featured an eagle with a swastika in its claws.

We were all happy to be back in our apartment, even if a few of our belongings had come up broken or missing. The important thing was we were all alive and unhurt. The only one who was missing was Papa, and Mutti was very sad about this, but tried not to show it.

Sirens

She did the best she could with what she had, which included the things we had been able to take with us when we had been evicted, and also those items we'd rescued from what the Americans had thrown out of the windows. We also retrieved the few small pieces of furniture we'd stored in the neighbor's barn.

Our mother tried her best to make our life as comfortable as possible. She and Frau Löber next door often traded favors and helped each other out. Besides Löber Oma, who lived with them on a permanent basis, three children were part of the Löber family, Christa was Mechthild's age and Hans Ulrich, who was called Uli by everyone, was two years older than I. The other son, Martin, was somewhere in between. Herr Löber hadn't returned from the war yet either at this time. Our two families had been good friends even before the war, and the members of my family were all sorry to see the Löbers leave later on when Herr Löber accepted the position of principal in a neighboring village, and they moved away into the school building in Langenaubach.

Before long our Oma decided it was time for her to return home. Although the trains still didn't run on a schedule, she felt she'd been gone from her home and her other daughter and her grandsons long enough. So she took a chance and, with several lengthy delays at different train stations, she made it back to her house safely. Tante Gertrud, Mutti's only sibling, along with her three sons, my cousins, who all lived with Oma, had been waiting anxiously and was happy to have her back.

Chapter 13
Life without Sirens

Mutti told me later, "It took a long time for me not to listen for the sound of the sirens. For weeks I had them on the edge of my consciousness, expecting to hear their terrible sound, that awful wailing, at any moment. I was always ready to escape into some kind of shelter."

Mechthild, too, had a difficult time adjusting to this new peace. "Whenever I heard the sound of an airplane, I ducked my head and felt like running for shelter while I waited for the impact of the bombs. It felt strange going to school and not having to worry about that any more."

As for me, I kind of missed the excitement, although I was glad not to be yanked out of bed to be hauled to the unfriendly environment of the basement. But, although I was still so young during the war, the feeling of wonder and, yes, relief at knowing that the war had ended, was very real. My problem was that I did not know what was to come next. Peace was not something I was familiar with and I was not sure what it entailed.

We tried to live our lives as normal as possible once the Americans had left our town, at least what our mother called normal. I didn't have any idea what normal was. When I asked Mechthild, she wasn't sure how to answer my question. It was not easy to switch your thinking from a war time setting to one of peace.

Mutti took care of the housework as before and tended her garden and Papa's bees. Mechthild was still stuck with me in the late afternoons and on weekends when she wasn't in school.

Although the trains ran only intermittently, she continued attending school in Dillenburg – on a more regular basis now. Since there were no more bombs, or

Sirens

the sirens that used to announce them to worry about, school wasn't called off early any more and she no longer had to walk that long trek home. She came home in late afternoon and I didn't get to see her all that much. I did resent the fact that I had to be in bed by 9 o'clock while she was allowed to stay up until 10.

With my sister gone quite a bit, Mutti had me attend Kindergarten which was something I had done during the war as well, but not very often. Our Kindergarten was not the same as what is called Kindergarten in America. Parents took their children there when they needed somebody to watch them. It could probably be compared to today's daycare centers. School always started with the first grade. Therefore, since Mutti was usually busy during the morning and Mechthild was off to school, it had been decided that I should attend Kindergarten on a regular basis. During the war Mutti had preferred to keep me as close to her as possible because there was always the worry in the back of her mind that something might happen; that the bombs would fall and the ladies in charge of us children would take care of themselves first and worry about the children they were supposed to take care of later. Whatever her reasons, she always felt better when she could keep an eye on me herself. But she did take me there when it was absolutely necessary.

The only Kindergarten in Allendorf was located at the upper edge of the village near the woods. I liked going there. I got to play with lots of children near my age, and there were games and coloring books and modeling clay to keep us entertained. Sometimes we did crafts, especially near the holidays such as Easter and Christmas.

We were taken for a walk every day when the weather was nice, sometimes right up to the forest. Mutti always sent a sandwich and some of her homemade juice with me, as did the mothers of the other children, and we would sit somewhere in the shade of a tree and eat our so-called second breakfast. Mutti regularly came to pick me up at noon and we walked down the village street toward home, and greeted people who were working around the outside of their houses. Sometimes we stopped at the butcher shop which was on the way, hoping they'd have some meat Mutti could cook for our lunch.

Like most children, I did not always behave myself and sometimes had to be punished. The usual punishment chosen by the lady who ran the Kindergarten was to lock unruly children into a room in the basement – the same one that served as their air-raid shelter– for a brief time, which was a fairly severe punishment in those days, considering that any basement was closely related to the threat of bombs in most people's thoughts, especially in the impressionable minds of small children.

On one particular day, when the war was still being fought all over Europe, I was waging my own mini war. I had been very angry when the lady placed me in the basement instead of the girl I'd been fighting with, because I felt the other girl had started the fight. I was about three years old at the time. When the Kindergarten lady came down to let me out of my "prison" I was gone. I had opened a small window and had escaped.

The helpers at the Kindergarten immediately started a search, going clear to the edge of the forest because they knew I liked it there. They feared I might have gotten lost among the trees. When they could no longer avoid it, one of them went to notify my mother. However, she had already discovered me – asleep, with my thumb in my mouth – in front of our apartment door for which I had no key. I'd made it all the way across town, from one end to the other, at the age of three, then through the main front door of our building, which was never kept locked during the day, and up the stairs. Mutti had been shopping and had found me on her

Sirens

return just a few minutes before the woman from the Kindergarten showed up.

*   *   *

During the war the small village of Allendorf boasted three bakeries, two butcher shops and five grocery stores. Having all these stores to choose from, however, did little good. Despite the ration cards we were issued, there was seldom anything available for purchase. After the war this changed gradually and stores were able to offer a little more by way of food merchandise. However, the stores didn't actually get stocked up completely until after the *Währungsreform* (currency reform) which took place on June 20, 1948, when all coins and banknotes underwent a complete change. No longer did we have to look at the swastika that had adorned all money in Germany during the Hitler years. At this same time every German citizen was allotted 60 *Deutsche Mark*.

I received my first piece of German candy at our neighborhood grocery store just down the street from us which my mother frequented almost exclusively. I was about five or six years old at the time. Mutti and I had gone shopping there and I was totally surprised when the man behind the counter, who was the owner of the store, reached into a jar and handed me something small that was wrapped in paper. I didn't know what I was holding in my hand and looked questioningly at Mutti who suggested, "Unwrap it and put it in your mouth." I did and it was so good. The grocer smiled when he saw the look on my face.

In the early days, when you went into a store, you had to wait your turn at any of these businesses and were waited on individually after the people who had been ahead of you had been helped. A couple of chairs or a wooden bench were generally provided for those who could not stand in line for any length of time. Flour and sugar and similar items were weighed to the customer's specifications after having been scooped from a large bin into a pointed paper bag.

The grocery store were Mutti did most of her shopping was located at the lower right of this building

I was always a little jealous of my friend Heidi whose mother bought Rama margarine. You got small, plastic animals with each pound you bought. They looked like they were made of glass and came in different colors, and Heidi had quite a collection of them. Mutti bought Sannella brand margarine, claiming it was better than Rama. That company only gave you little stamps with flowers and plants on them that you could paste into a small album which you received after accumulating a certain number of points. I was not at all interested in those, but I could not convince my mother to switch from Sannella to Rama.

Service was the same at the butcher shop as in the grocery store. You waited your turn and when you told the butcher what kind of meat you wanted and how much, he cut off the required piece. The butcher shop was a little farther away, about halfway to the top of the

Sirens

village. The butcher always gave me a small piece of smoked sausage about two inches long, which I ate on the way home, without bread, which was a no-no at our meals because Mutti considered it wasteful. When Mutti decided I was old enough to go to the butcher shop by myself, she'd send me, after handing me a shopping bag with her billfold in a side pocket, which contained roughly the amount of money I would need, and a shopping list. I still received my piece of sausage which was sometimes substituted by a piece from a ring of bologna. I don't remember ever being given anything free at the bakery.

One time Tante Gertrud came for a rare visit. Her husband never did return from the war. He was killed in action, she was told. Now the two sisters, she and Mutti, decided to get their minds off their problems (Papa hadn't come home yet at this time) and they walked to Haiger to do some shopping in the stores that were gradually starting to come back to that bombed-out town, at first into buildings that had been spared by the bombs, later in newly erected ones. On their way home, already in the outskirts of town, the two women spotted a butcher shop displaying a string of small sausages hanging in the shop windows. Tante Gertrud saw all the mouthwatering meat and told Mutti, "Let's go in. I haven't had any good beef sausages for a very long time. Come on, let's buy some."

Mutti couldn't figure out why the butcher gave the two of them such strange looks when he heard my aunt's request for two pounds of beef sausages, but he weighed them, wrapped them up and handed them to her. After she'd paid and they'd left the store and had crossed the street, Mutti looked back to see what the name of the butcher shop was. That's when she discovered something very disturbing. The legend above the shop window stated in large black letters: "Schmidt's Horse Butcher Shop." I don't know if Tante Gertrud ever ate her sausages.

At about this same time a rumor was making the rounds, warning people not to buy canned meat because the cans might contain human flesh.

It seemed strange to be going to all the places where we did our shopping without having to worry about the sirens starting up and then having to rush home to our basement or find a shelter nearby. Even at my young age I noticed the difference and felt more carefree. But after the initial joyful excitement over the war now being a thing of the past, Mutti didn't act very happy. She missed Papa. We knew he was a prisoner of war and, since she had started to receive occasional letters from him, we also knew that he was still alive – but when would he be allowed to return to us?

Sirens

Chapter 14
Papa Comes Home

    Although I was only a little over four years old, I could tell that Mutti was worried about something other than the ever-present threat of bombs that we still had to content with for a while before Papa would return home; however, she wouldn't tell Mechthild or me what was bothering her, even after I asked her. "It's nothing," she said. "I'm sure it will be alright in the end." This took place a few months before the war had ended and the bombers were a constant presence, making us go to the basement as many as five times throughout the night as well as several times during the daytime. One day Mechthild told me that Mutti hadn't received a letter from Papa for a very long time and a lot of her daily letters to him had been returned to her. "She's afraid Papa has been killed during the fighting," Mechthild informed me.

    Then, one day, Mutti was notified that Papa was alive but was a prisoner of war. He was being held by the Americans somewhere in France. It was a great relief to her to get this news. Now she could only hope that nothing would happen to him before the war ended. Of course, she continued to worry about him, but not to the earlier degree.

    At war's end many of the other soldiers who lived in Allendorf began to return home from where ever they'd been held as POWs, or from where they had been fighting at the front, but Papa was not among them.

    One night, a few weeks after the end of the war, I was awakened by a strange noise. I lay in my bed for a moment to make sure I hadn't been dreaming. I hadn't because I heard it again. The noise sounded as though it was coming from the window. Although I was a little afraid, I was also curious and hopped out of bed, ran around the foot of the bed and along Mechthild's side where the window was located. Then I peeked through the sheer curtains.

What I saw scared me even more. The bright moonlight revealed a man in a gray German uniform who seemed to be looking straight at me. But I knew, since I was on the second floor and there was no light on in the room, it was not possible for him to see me. After a while he bent over and picked something up off the ground which I could see him toss toward the window. And there was that noise again. I heard it just as the object touched the window glass.

That's when I lost it. I ran into Mutti's bedroom through the connecting door and shouted, "Mutti, Mutti, there is a strange man standing in the yard throwing rocks at our window." The war had left all the German people, including the children, somewhat nervous and prone to overreact when unexpected events occurred. It had also left them with the ability to wake up at a moment's notice.

Although she had been in a deep sleep, Mutti sat straight up in bed swinging her legs over the side and, at the same time, reaching for her robe. Although she didn't know what to make of my announcement, she decided to investigate. Since her side window was separated from ours only by the wall between the two bedrooms, she had the same view from there that I had from our room. What she saw below made her exclaim in surprise, "Ursula," she almost shouted while quickly opening the window, "That's not a strange man down there; that's your Papa!"

It was June 21, 1945. I was not quite four and a half years old when I, knowingly, saw my father for the first time – and I did not like what I saw.

Traveling through parts of France and half of Germany, two war-torn countries, through the rubble of bomb-ravaged towns, over demolished houses and roads that had not yet been cleared of the debris, sometimes also by railroad, he'd been in a great hurry to get home and hadn't worried about how he looked. He just wanted to see his wife and children again – as soon as he possibly could.

Papa hadn't taken a key to the front door of the building with him, and since it was kept locked at night, he couldn't get in. Not wanting to wake up anyone else in the building, he had been trying to get Mutti's attention by throwing small pebbles at her bedroom window. But with the windows so close together, he'd missed a few times and had hit ours instead, waking me up in the process. Since the war was over and the worry about the bombs a thing of the past, and working so hard every day, Mutti had been sleeping deeply and hadn't heard the pebbles hit the glass. But she had jumped up quickly when she'd heard my loud voice, fearing another catastrophe had come to claim us. Now she rushed downstairs in her robe to let her husband in, a husband she hadn't seen for a very long time and had, at one point, almost given up for dead. As soon as he came through the door she threw her arms around him to give him a huge hug, although she had to reach up high since he was so much taller than she. But he pushed her away gently, "Wife," he said, "I'm covered with lice. Let's hug after I've had a chance to take a long hot bath."

I had roused Mechthild, and the two of us were waiting anxiously at the door to our apartment. We could hear our parents below talk from this spot, but were unable to see them because of the stairs. "I can't wait to see Papa," she whispered to me. "I'm so glad he's finally come home." I had mixed feelings about this man everybody said was my father.

Up close, despite being in uniform, the man who entered our home at Mutti's side looked like a bum. He was dirty, unshaven, needed a haircut and smelled badly. At 6 foot, 2 inches he towered over Mutti who was only 5 foot, 1 inch tall. He sure didn't look like what I thought my Papa would look like judging by the pictures of him I had studied from time to time.

I don't remember much about the rest of the night. We were sent back to bed while Mutti and Papa talked in the kitchen. I could hear them but could not make out what they were saying. But I could hear the happiness in both of their voices.

It was too late to get the stove going and it would take much too long to heat enough water for a bath. Mutti told us later that Papa had refused to get into the bed with her but slept on the floor instead because of the lice.

The next few days were difficult for me. I wasn't used to having a man around the house, and I didn't much like it. Also, I didn't want to share Mutti with him and so I sulked, although I could tell how happy she now was. Mutti finally told me that I might as well get used to it because Papa was there to stay.

It actually didn't take long for me to become accustomed to Papa being in our life. It was he who kindled my interest in reading, which led to my love of writing, because he was the one who now read to me the fairy tales I so loved. Even after the war had ended, Mutti rarely had time to read to me, but she had made sure that I would always have those stories around, because she had stuffed our large volume of "Grimm's Fairy Tales" amongst the bedding when we'd had to abandon our apartment. She'd slipped it into a pillow case to make sure it wouldn't get lost.

Papa now took the time to read to me every day, and I savored each minute of our reading experiences. I could never get enough of the stories and kept begging him for more. After a while Papa got a little tired of my constant nagging to have stories read to me. Also, as the days passed and he fitted himself back into the civilian life, he became busier. For one thing he took over the chore of taking care of the bees again, sparing Mutti all that extra work. Finally he informed me that

Sirens

I was old enough now to learn to read and he proceeded to teach me – not a big issue for him since he was a teacher. It wasn't long before I no longer had to ask him to read to me because I could do it for myself whenever I wanted. However, I missed the togetherness we'd had during our reading sessions.

After that, there were many times when my father caught me reading in bed long after my designated bedtime. Since one of the panels in my bedroom door was made of milk glass, anybody who walked down or across the hallway could see if my light was on. So I found a flashlight and read under the covers – probably ruining my eyes for life. Papa soon caught onto that trick, and put a stop to it by checking on me regularly before he retired for the night along with the rest of the family..

When I started school at the age of six, the teacher had nothing left to teach me when it came to reading and writing, and I was quite bored during those classes.

*   *   *

It seems to be an unwritten rule that life can't stay happy forever, and our peaceful existence ended when Papa decided he had to go back to work, and that he was ready to teach again. But, the town's government wouldn't allow him go back to teaching, at least not in Allendorf. They had other ideas about my father and informed him that, since he had been a Nazi, he was not fit to teach any of the town's children. But since he had to get some kind of a job in order for us to continue to get ration cards, he went to the forest for a time and worked as a lumberjack. He was paid a small salary and was also given wood, some of which he was able to trade for the things we needed, such as some food we could not get with the ration cards. The good part about this was that Mutti no longer had to pull the

Ursula (Winter) Turner

little hand wagon into the woods to look for branches that could be used for fire wood.

Papa worked in the woods for a year and a half. That's how long it took for his case to be processed at the government trials, at which time he was finally able to tell everybody his side of the story and that he had not been a Nazi by choice, but that he had been forced onto this position by threats. He'd been told that he only had two worthless daughters who could not become the soldiers that were needed to fight for the Reich, and that Mechthild and I, and perhaps even Mutti, would be killed if he did not commit to becoming a member of the Nazi party. This had left him no alternative. Even though he disliked Hitler and his policies and politics tremendously, he ended up a Nazi with no obvious choice in the matter.

His superiors in the army found my father to be very intelligent and therefore ordered him to attend officer's school. Well, Papa was, indeed, intelligent and flunked the classes on purpose. He had no desire to become one of Hitler's officers. And he was proud to be able to tell us that throughout the war he had managed to avoid shooting at any human being. He only shot at targets. (I never saw him with a gun.) He was very happy to have been entnazifiziert (denazified), and he was glad when he was told that he'd be going back to teaching again as soon as the new school year started.

During the time when Papa worked as a wood cutter, we could not live in our apartment above the schoolrooms which meant, we had to move once again. This time it was much easier. For one thing, Papa was there to help; also there was no two-hour deadline. Therefore, we were able to take all of our belongings, including the furniture, which was hauled to our new apartment in a neighbor's wagon that was pulled by his two cows. Papa and Mutti had found an upstairs apartment in the house of an older farm couple who lived at the edge of town, making Mechthild's walk to the train station in Haiger a little shorter. The couple's daughter had gotten married not long before this time and their son had been killed in the war, leaving the house nearly empty and with plenty of room for our family. Papa paid part of the rent with wood and also helped Herr Weber with the farm whenever he could.

There was one thing I hated about this new place; it had an outhouse that was inhabited by a number of creepy, crawly things, including spiders. Although spiders in Germany are not poisonous, I was afraid of those hairy-looking, many-legged creatures. I had used the outhouse at both of my grandparent's homes and had hated them. But I had known that it was only temporary and that we would be returning to our indoor toilet. This one at the Weber's house might be long-term. I preferred the flushable toilet at our old apartment.

One day, when I was done with my business in the outhouse and was ready to step outside, I discovered that a very fat spider had settled down on the hook that locked the door. There was no way I was going to touch that hook with the spider sitting on it, and the thing refused to move. I stood frozen for a moment, then took a deep breath and began to scream at the top of my lungs. Mutti happened to be in the yard and when she heard my screams she came running. Relieved that nothing serious had happened to me, she tried to talk me into taking a piece of the newspaper we used for toilet paper and knock the spider off the hook with it. Nothing doing. I stayed as far back from the hairy thing as I could, hoping I wouldn't step into the territory of another one that might be waiting behind me. Herr Weber finally came to the rescue. Using an axe he knocked the door down enough to allow me to exit my self-imposed prison. He wasn't any too pleased at the damage and Papa had to fix the door after he came home from the woods.

The outhouse is one of only two things I can remember about our stay at the Weber's house that left an impression with me. Another incident, or rather a number of them, has also stayed in my mind. It was the eating of peanut butter day after day. We did an awful lot of that while living in the Weber house. We had brought the peanut butter with us from the school where the Americans had left it in our pantry. We'd never heard of peanut butter before the time of the American occupation and found it quite tasty – at first. But we ate so much of it since there wasn't much else, that I finally couldn't stand it any more, and to this day I will not touch it. I haven't learned to like spiders in the intervening years either.

After Papa's trial, where he was cleared of all charges brought against him, we were able to leave the Weber's house and move back to our old apartment in the school building where Papa and I started school at the same time, he as a fifth and sixth grade teacher and I as a first grade student.

Sirens

Chapter 15
Refugees Crowd Our Building

By the time we were allowed to move back to our apartment above the classrooms, the same one we had occupied before, the building was bursting at the seams due to all the people now living there. They were a part of the many refugees who had fled from the eastern parts of Germany and Eastern Europe toward the West, ahead of the Russians whom they so feared. They were trying to get away from the soldiers of the Red Army who committed so many cruelties and inflicted such unimaginable atrocities on the civilian population of Germany. They made no distinction in whom they raped – from young girls to old women – all were fair game to them. In addition, they tortured many of the male citizens of our country, often shooting them afterward if they didn't die from their injuries.

Many Ethnic Germans who had made their homes in Hungary, Czechoslovakia and other eastern European countries were now seeking places to live while they attempted to get their lives put together again. Many had decided to leave their homes voluntarily because they would soon be occupied by the Russians anyway; however, numerous families were expelled by force and had to leave what they had considered their home, in advance of the Russian army. The first were called *Flüchtlinge* (refugees), the second received the name *Heimatvertriebene* (expellees). Most didn't own much more than the clothes on their backs although a few had managed to haul small carts loaded with as many of their belongings as they would hold.

There were others who had lost their homes during the bombings of the cities where they had lived until then. All of these people were in need of homes, and some of them found one in our school building.

Ursula (Winter) Turner

With so many buildings in these larger cities destroyed by the bombs, living space was at a premium and many of the refugees continued on to smaller towns in hopes of finding what they thought of as a provisional home, until they could get back on their feet. So, our school was once more chosen for a purpose it had not been designed for, although classes were held once again. A number of the fleeing families found what was supposed to be temporary lodgings there although, as it turned out, their stay stretched into several years.

*   *   *

The school building

The building had always had two levels of attic. One was on the same level as the two small apartments intended for single teachers, with the attic space on either side of them. The second attic was above this level and could be reached by a short, straight set of steps. Each apartment had, besides a kitchen/living room combination and a bedroom, also a toilet with lavatory. But in order for the occupants to reach this toilet, they had to cross a small part of the attic with the toilet located directly across from their apartment door.

When we returned to the school, the side on the left of the stairs was still the same as far as the attic went, although it had been divided into several smaller sections that were to be used by the newcomers. A German family, who had been living in America throughout the war and had just recently been able to return, lived in the apartment on that side. They were made up of a grandmother, parents and a son and daughter. They kept pretty much to themselves and I did not get to know them very well. However, the son let me borrow some comic books he had brought from America. I loved to look at the pictures of Donald Duck and his three nephews, and Uncle Scrooge, but was frustrated that I could not read the words since they were in English.

The other apartment was occupied by Frau Schol, her son Hermann, and her daughter, my deaf friend, Rosel. Herr Schol had been killed in the war early on.

The two young teachers for whom these two apartments had been intended were from Allendorf and preferred to live in town with their families.

The attic on Frau Schol's side had been turned into two one-room apartments that began on the other side of the last set of stairs that led to the uppermost floor. The first room was crowded with seven occupants. There were Herr and Frau Meyer, their adult son and daughter and the daughter's husband along with their two toddlers. I heard my first cuss words from Herr Meyer. Perhaps he was entitled, but I suspect they were not new to him.

"Only" five people lived in the room around the corner from the first one. Frau Sieber, another woman who had lost her husband in the war, her two daughters, Fanni, who was Mechthild's age and Heidi, who was my age, and two sons in between, Donsch and Ede. Heidi ended up becoming my best friend during our growing-up years until first her family, then mine, moved to different towns. I have lost track of her through the years and don't know where to find her today.

All of the people in those two rooms shared the Schol family's toilet facilities since they lived on that side. Frau Schol often complained that the Meyers never shared in the cleaning. The Dieters, the family from America, were the only ones to use the other toilet.

Living one floor below, we had extra tenants as well. No sooner had we moved back to the school, when our family was asked, or rather, ordered, to give up one of the rooms in our apartment to be used by refugees. The Löbers had to do the same thing. We gave up our dining room which was closest to the apartment door. This meant that, when the strangers moved in, they would not have to walk through the rest of our apartment but could leave theirs by simply crossing the end of the long hall to the door that led to the stairs. We rarely used this room anyway. We liked to eat our meals in the living room in winter and in the kitchen in summer.

Our tenants consisted of an elderly man, Herr Kauer, and his two middle-aged spinster daughters, Mitzi and Dolfi, who were as different from each other as night and day to use an old cliché. Mitzi had a dark complexion with dark hair showing some gray, and she was very thin. Dolfi, the older one of the two, had gray hair that looked as though it had been blond in her younger years, and she was fairly stout. The one thing that fascinated me about Dolfi was a large goiter that grew at the front of her neck. All three of our new neighbors were very likable. They were clean and industrious. The ladies often went to the woods to gather, not only blueberries like we still did because we liked them and took many trips to the woods to collect them, war or no war, but they also went after wild strawberries, hazelnuts and mushrooms. Mutti couldn't tell the poisonous variety from the others so had always left all mushrooms alone. The Kauer ladies let me taste some after they'd been cooked but I couldn't stand the slimy things. Maybe it was the way they fixed them because I enjoy them today.

The Löbers had also given up their dining room. They had to share their living quarters with an elderly couple, the Pelinkas. Herr Pelinka had been a teacher before the war, but the ordeal of fleeing from the Russians had left him too ill to continue in this profession. He was actually past retirement age, but many of the refugees had to work anyway in order to put food on their table. I think this genteel couple got some help from the new government. They kept pretty much to themselves and we didn't see a lot of them.

The Meyers were very dirty people. Every time I walked past their door on my way to visit my friend, Heidi, I held my nose because of the awful odor coming from their room. And if a member of the Meyer family happened to step out just then and opened the door, the smell just about knocked me over. I couldn't understand how they could live like that day in and day out. I always hurried past their door as fast I could until I had made it into the Sieber's room which always smelled clean, although sometimes I detected cooking odors that were not familiar to me.

One day Mutti discovered little red spots all over her that were itching something fierce, she said. After a few days of trying to discover what was causing her discomfort, the mystery was solved. When she changed the sheets one day, she found little black dots, bedbugs, all over her white bedding. The Meyer's room happened to be partly above the bedroom of my parents, and those awful little bugs had come down through the walls and had attacked my mother. Mutti was mortified. She always kept our apartment super clean and for her to have bedbugs was just too much. Papa, who for some reason had been spared by the little insects, visited the terminator and asked him to treat our apartment. He then had a word or two with Her Meyer about cleanliness. Herr Meyer swore under his breath, Papa said, and stomped away. Nothing changed and the bugs returned several more times until Papa insisted the Meyers have their room sprayed as well.

At one point the community of Allendorf decided to give the refugee families a helping hand. They chose a piece of land on the other side of the valley, across the creek and the highway, up the hill, under the railroad overpass and a little farther on. This was divided into small parcels of land and each refugee family who lived in Allendorf was deeded one of these plots to be used for a garden space where they could grow vegetables and herbs.

Most of the refugees made use of this land. Many erected small sheds in which they kept their gardening tools so they wouldn't have to carry them back and forth such a long distance, and they built fences around their small gardens to keep the wild animals, such as rabbits and deer, out. I often went with Heidi and her mother, not so much to help, but to have Heidi's company.

I will never forget something we saw on one of our trips, and kept seeing each time we visited the Sieber's garden plot after that. Times were still pretty rough during these first weeks and months of the postwar era and many people's feelings had been hardened by the war. But what we saw that first day was utterly cruel. Heidi spotted it first and pointed it out to her mother and me. As we emerged from under the railroad overpass she noticed that somebody had hung the body of a dog on a branch of a tall bush that grew along the railroad embankment. Frau Sieber forbade us to touch it and even told us not to look at it. But on each subsequent trip we couldn't help but notice how this poor animal's carcass was wasting away until there was nothing left but a skeleton. Not one soul bothered to cut the dog down and give it a burial, not even Heidi's mother. People minded their own business back then, having it ingrained by the years under Hitler because, if you didn't, you could bring a lot of trouble onto yourself and your family. Also, I guess, during this period of time people had more important things to worry about. However, the incident left a lasting impression in my mind. Both Heidi and I tried to imagine how anybody could be so cruel, not only to the animal, but to all of the people who had to pass the spot and could not help but see it.

*   *   *

All of the German citizens who had been forced to flee Eastern Europe because of the Russian occupation of their former homes eventually received large monetary compensations by the new German government to cover some of their losses. In addition, they were offered low-interest building loans to induce them to have homes built for them. This served two purposes, it relieved some of the crowded conditions of many homes, and it was a part of the rebuilding of Germany from the war damages.

One by one the refugee families left their cramped quarters in the Allendorf school building and moved into their own brand new homes that had been built to their specifications. Finally they were able to lead normal lives again and enjoy the space that many of them had been doing without. This, however, took place over the course of several years which allowed Heidi and me to spend a big part of our childhood together. When Rosel came home during her vacations from deaf school, we became a threesome. Other girls from the neighborhood including Elsa and Elisabeth also joined us frequently, but the three of us, living in the same house, got together quite often. Heidi and I had quickly picked up the sign language as Rosel was teaching it to us and we had no problem communicating with her. My dilemma was that my family spent so many of our vacations at my grandparents' farm, allowing me little time to spend with my friends.

*My childhood friends,
Elsa and Heidi*

*Rosel and Elisabeth
were also my friends*

Although I was sad when Heidi's family finally did move into their own house, I was also happy for her. That one-room apartment she'd had to share with her siblings and her mother had to be an awful way to live. They had divided the room in half for privacy, with curtains they'd made out of bed sheets. The front part of the room contained their living quarters, with the kitchen on the left and the living room on the side where the windows were located. On the left side of the door sat a small cabinet that held pots and pans. Frau Sieber kept a bucket of water on it as well as her dishpan. The water had to be carried from the communal lavatory. The stove and a larger cabinet for dishes completed the kitchen. A sofa stood against the wall on the living room side of the door, with a table in front of it and some chairs around it. This was where the family members ate their meals. Another, larger, cabinet stood against one side of the wall which was made of sheets.

The part of the room behind the curtains was the "bedroom." It was, again, divided for the purpose of privacy between the males and females of the family, with the boys each in their own single bed on one side, and Frau Sieber in her own bed on the other side, while Heidi and Fanni had to share one next to her. My friend and her family were forced to live this way for several years. When they arrived in Allendorf they had no other possessions than what they could carry. Most of their furniture had been donated to them. The only good part I could find when I visited their living quarters was the terrific view they were able to enjoy from their third-floor windows. I did have a crush on Ede, the younger one of Heidi's brothers.

Since the Siebers had decided to build their new house in Haiger, I didn't see much of Heidi and her family after they moved.

Herr Kauer died before he was able to leave the school building. Mitzi and Dolfi got to enjoy their new home, which was also located in Haiger, for a number of years. I don't believe either of them ever married. Dolfi, with her goiter, would probably have had a difficult time finding a man. I'm certain Mitzi stayed with her out of loyalty for her sister.

The Pelinkas moved in with younger relatives they had miraculously been able to unearth somewhere in another part of Germany. With all the uncertainties of the postwar years, and with so many documents destroyed either through bomb damage or for other reasons, it was difficult to locate anyone for the first several years after the war. The International Red Cross assisted people in finding their families; however, some never did locate their loved ones and were unable to determine if they were alive or dead, so the Pelinkas were fortunate to have found their relatives.

I never did learn what happened to the Dieters. They were simply gone one day as I found out when I came home from school. Perhaps they returned to America.

Frau Schol lived out her last few years away from the school as well. After both of her children had married and moved to neighboring towns (Rosel had found a young man who was also deaf), she moved in with a sister. Both of those apartments remained empty for several years.

Herr Löber, after returning home from the war unharmed, accepted the position of principal at the school in Langenaubach, six kilometers (3 ¼ miles) away from Allendorf. We never warmed up much to his replacement and his family. They were a bit standoffish and acted like they were better than the rest of us since they came from a big city.

After Herr Löber left, Papa was promoted and became principal of the school in Allendorf. He, additionally, taught seventh and eighth grade.

Today nobody lives in the school building. It has been renovated and modernized with a wing built in the area where Mutti's garden used to be. Since the town has almost doubled in population, many more children attend school and extra classrooms were needed. Our old apartment has been turned into specialty classrooms and storage areas.

Sirens

Chapter 16
Going to School

The school building in Allendorf was set up to teach the town's children through eight grades, with two grades placed together into each of the four classrooms. The classrooms opened into a large central hall or lobby. On one end of this hall was a small door that led into the residential part of the building. Two large doors opposite this were used by the students and led down a wide set of stairs into the schoolyard.

The schoolyard of my childhood cannot, by any stretch of the imagination, be compared to today's schoolyards where children spent their recess. Ours consisted of a large, fenced-in area that was covered with gravel. There was no playground equipment of any kind, nor were there benches to sit on while we ate our second breakfast. The fence was built on top of a low brick wall, and we sat on the edge of the bricks that extended from under the fence boards. School was held from 8 in the morning until 1 in the afternoon, Mondays through Saturdays. Since our school days were shorter than they are in this country, we were allowed one ten-minute break to spend outdoors, long enough to have a snack, the aforementioned second breakfast. We brought this from home and it consisted of a lunchmeat or cheese sandwich (no peanut butter), and whatever our mothers had packed for us to drink. I could have gone upstairs and had mine in our apartment, but as always, I wanted to be like the other kids. We were always home in time for lunch, although we ate at 1 o'clock rather than noon. Consequently we didn't have supper until six o'clock. Since my dad had the same hours I had, Mutti always timed our cooked meal for right after school was out and we ate sandwiches, always open-faced, at the evening meal. Instead of bread and butter plates, we used little boards, especially made for this, to fix them on.

The students' toilets were located in a small building at the bottom of the schoolyard which contained a small stable at the other end, where a family, who lived in the neighborhood, kept a few goats and rabbits. I always ran upstairs to our apartment and used our own toilet. Although I wanted to be like the other kids, I drew a line when it came to using something that, to me, was too much like an outdoor toilet.

Getting to my classroom would have been simple for me. After leaving the apartment, I descended the same flight of stairs we had so often hurried down during the air-raids. But now, after reaching the bottom, instead of turning right toward the basement door, I could have opened the door on my left which led directly into the school's central hallway. The first and second grade classroom was located to my immediate right after entering the lobby.

However, in this case I, once more, wanted to be like the other kids. So, after I arrived downstairs, I turned right instead of left and exited by way of the front door. I then turned left, walked along the front of the building until I reached the entrance to the schoolyard and there joined the other children who were waiting for the bell to ring. At this point, we had to line up by classes and enter the building in an orderly fashion by ascending the wide staircase first, then walking through the big doors where the teachers were waiting to lead us toward our classrooms. However, if the weather was bad and it was either raining or freezing cold, I preferred to use the inside access to my classroom – one of the perks of living in the building.

We had no lockers and therefore carried all of our books, pencils, slate and other school supplies we would need during class in a square leather backpack that fit in a compartment under our desktops. The backpacks could be opened to get our supplies out without having to be removed.

In the first grade, which is when school begins for the children in Germany, since Kindergarten is voluntary, we didn't need much by way of supplies. We used a slate that was actually made from slate and had a wooden frame. It had a sponge and drying cloth tied to a hole in this frame. These hung out of our backpack on one side at the top to keep the sponge from getting everything else in the backpack wet. We also had a stylus that was made especially to write on the slate. I carried several of these writing instruments in a wooden box similar to a pencil box. When Papa sharpened my stylus each evening with his pocket knife, it always made me shiver and gave me goose bumps because of the noise it made. Anything we wrote on the slate could be wiped off with the wet sponge. The cloth was used to dry the slate, of course. We also had a reader and a book with simple math problems.

Our teacher, Fräulein Ströhmann, was a gray-haired, skinny spinster who wore her hair severely scraped back from her face, then braided and twisted into a bun which she wore at the nape of her neck. She always wore calf or ankle length dresses, as did most women of that era. I don't remember my mother ever wearing anything but dresses or skirts.

Fräulein Ströhmann always looked very stern, and she used to get quite upset with me and often complained to Papa because I didn't pay attention during reading and spelling class. He explained to her that I was probably bored because I already knew how to do those things, but she insisted that I pay attention anyway. The math lessons, in turn, gave me all kinds of problems. I never did have a head for numbers – still don't and have a difficult time balancing my checkbook.

Ursula (Winter) Turner

My first grade teacher Fraulein Strömann and Papa who was teaching fourth grade at this time.

My classmates and I ended up attending first grade for one and a half years. We started school in spring, but during that summer, the school board decided to change that and have school start in fall instead. However, they didn't feel that half a year was long enough for us to attend first grade, so we had to wait until school started the following year before we got moved up to the next grade. I guess all the kids in the higher classes had the same problem.

We remained in the same classroom for second grade, but sat in the back of the room while the new first graders sat in the front. We were now considered old enough and adequately acquainted with the ways of school life that we received corporal punishment if the teacher felt it was warranted because we had broken a rule. After we had misbehaved, we were made to stand in the front of the classroom, hold out our hand, palm up, to allow Fräulein Ströhmann to give us several hard whacks by means of a very thin stick, and the worse the misdeed had been, the more whacks we were given. This sure stung, but our teacher made certain that we always stuck out our left hand so as not to damage our working hand. Natural left-handers were forced to use their right hand in those days, so it was the same for all. As first graders, we had occupied the front rows of the classroom and had been close enough to see the consequences students faced if they did not behave. Now the new first graders got a good look at what they would be facing by way of punishment if they didn't toe the line during their next school year.

In the second grade, needle craft was added to the girls' curriculum. We learned to sew simple things such as pin cushions and sheaths for our scissors, which we made from felt with a blanket stitch placed around the edges of the projects to hold them together. There was still a shortage of goods, and my felt was the color of an American Army uniform and had pink edgings made from embroidery floss my mother supplied. I don't remember what the boys did during this hour. I know it wasn't needlecraft. That was considered unmanly at the time.

When I was promoted to third grade it meant moving to the classroom next door and being taught by a different instructor. Fräulein Wolfram was younger and prettier than Fräulein Ströhmann. She wasn't as strict either.

As before, we started out at the front of the room, with the girls on one side of the aisle and the boys on the other. This grade gave me my first experience of writing with ink. All students had to bring a small bottle of ink which was placed in the inkwell of our desk. We used a pen that had to be dipped into the ink repeatedly in order to be able to continue with our writing projects. I used blotting paper frequently, not only to blot my work dry, but also for the many ink spots that frequently found their way onto my work sheets. I never received a good grade in penmanship.

Ursula (Winter) Turner

Fräulein Wolfram was supposed to continue as my fourth-grade teacher as well, but she either quit or was transferred to another school. At any rate, my fourth grade teacher turned out to be none other than my very own Papa. All the kids in my class envied me, assuming that I would now have it made. Having my own father as a teacher surely would make this year easy for me. How wrong they were.

*   *   *

Papa was probably the strictest teacher I had to put up with throughout my schooling. He felt that, as his daughter, I had to set an example for the other students and, by golly, he'd make sure that I did. I felt on many occasions that he picked on me and often complained to Mutti, but she took his side and agreed with anything he did.

Although he was my father and I called him Papa at home, I had to address him as Herr Winter or Herr *Lehrer* (teacher) when we were in the classroom. At first this felt awkward to me, but eventually I got used to it. I even slipped sometimes and called him Herr Winter after school.

Being around me at home all the time, Papa was very familiar with all of my bad habits. One of them was twisting a strand of my hair around my finger when I was preoccupied and sucking my thumb. I did this especially when I was reading something. Papa made sure to embarrass me in front of the entire class several times by stopping whatever he was doing, looking at me, and then saying in a loud voice, "Stop twisting your hair, Ursula, and take that thumb out of your mouth. If you continue this you will soon be bald and have teeth like a rabbit," and he did this several times during the day. I know he was trying to break me of this habit by humiliating me in front of my friends and classmates and some of the girls did giggle while the boys just grinned. Sadly, I have to report that his efforts did not succeed. Far from it. I still twirl my hair around my finger when I'm reading, and I'm past retirement age now. Luckily, I did finally stop sucking my thumb, but, later on, substituted cigarettes. When I quit that nasty habit some years ago, I filled the void with food. I've often wondered if all this isn't some kind of a security blanket I still feel in need of due to the war years.

I did learn a lot of things in the fourth grade, however, and I am not just referring to the subjects of study that Papa tried to plant into our nearly empty heads. One very important thing I was taught was to pay attention, even though this took a little while to take hold. In the beginning I often didn't listen when we were given our homework assignments. I mistakenly assumed I could wait until after I got home and then ask Papa what work we were to do. The first time Papa sat next to me at the dinner table when I asked him. He got this sad look in his eyes, making me think that I must have disappointed him somehow. His answer surprised me, although, knowing my father, it shouldn't have, "I'm sorry, Ursula," he replied to my request, "but how would I know what homework assignments you have? I am your father." And he remained firm in his answer, no matter how hard I tried to wheedle it out of him. No begging or pleading would get him to relent and tell me what my assignments were. When we were at home, he was my father, not my teacher. I often ran upstairs to ask Heidi, who sat next to me in class. But she didn't always pay attention either. In fact, there was a time, or two, when Papa had threatened to separate us because we were always whispering to each other. So, a few times I ended up going to school without having done my homework, and Papa would not hesitate to give me a 5 (F) for this. I did, eventually, learn my lesson and paid better attention.

Ursula (Winter) Turner

When I did do my homework I always sat at a small table that was placed against the wall under the windows. My gaze often strayed from my ink-blotted pages out onto the street and the goings-on there. One sight I really enjoyed. This was watching the cows come home during the warmer months of the year. I knew that every morning during those months, the cowherd went from farm house to farm house throughout the village to collect all the cows that would not be needed by their owner for any work that day. He and his two dogs herded them through the town's streets and up to the high meadow that belonged to the community, where they spent the day grazing. In the evening he brought them back home. The farmers could hear their return from a distance, because each cow had a bell tied around her neck, and get ready to receive them. Elsa's dad across the street from us owned two cows, and the cowherd often stopped at their house to pick them up and then deliver them again. One big disadvantage of this daily event was the cow patties left all along the streets. But we were used to that and stepped around them. The street sweeper, not a machine but a man, would eventually take care of them.

Not only did Papa pick on me, or at least so I thought, but he was much stricter with me than he was with my classmates for such things as whispering to a friend, passing notes, or not paying attention in general. He always called my name out loud, and sometimes I had to stand in the corner. The others soon noticed this and stopped envying me for having my father as a teacher.

Papa expected my handwriting to be perfect, but no matter how hard I tried, I could not get past the ink blots, nor could I get the letters to look neat and even. He took penmanship seriously and would not let us write with ballpoint pens when they first appeared on the scene because, in his opinion, they smeared, which was true. With math being my weakest subject, it was

Sirens

his strongest, and I could never please him with my math accomplishments.

During the summer months the cowherd stopped by each farm house in the mornings to see if they needed their cows. If they had no use for them that day, he herded them down the town's streets toward the community meadow and then brought them back home in the evening.

The cowherd with his two dogs guarding the cows on the meadow.

The fourth grade seemed to last forever, but I do believe I learned a lot when Papa was my teacher.
   Mechthild had Papa for a teacher before the war, and she felt the same way I did.

*   *   *

   After the fourth grade my school life changed drastically. One day, during the last few weeks toward the end of the school year I went to Haiger to be tested for my eligibility to attend middle school which, in Germany, starts after the fourth grade, but only for those who pass the test. Those who want to attend middle school but didn't pass the test are given a second chance. They can attempt to take the test again after they've finished fifth grade, which will put them a year behind if they do manage to pass, but has them continue through the eight grades of elementary school if they don't pass. I was lucky and passed on the first go-around.
   Starting with the following school year I attended the middle school in Haiger.
   Now there was no more going down a set of stairs to get to school in bad weather, or walking around the building trying to be like the other students when the sun was shining. I now *was* like the other students. There were no others, at least not from my class, attending this new school with me. None of my fellow students had chosen to attend middle school and, later, high school and college. All of them were satisfied to learn a trade or join their parents in their business as apprentices.
   Papa received a promotion at about this same time and was made principal of the school in Allendorf. He now taught seventh and eighth grade.
   There were no school buses in Germany then. To get to school I would have had to take a public bus, except that they weren't running yet due to the war, or

walk, or I could ride my bicycle. In the summer, going by bike was fine unless it stormed, when I usually arrived at school soaking wet in spite of the rain gear I wore which was evidently not much use on a bike. But a bicycle was out of the question in our cold and snowy winters, and my parents did not own a car, nor did either of them ever drive one. So I walked. But then a savvy entrepreneur who owned a Volkswagen bus came up with the idea to give students from area villages a break while earning a little extra money for himself. Using his little bus he made the rounds of the towns, which are seldom more than 3 or 4 kilometers (1 ¾ or 2 ½ miles) apart from each other in Germany, and hauled the students to the school in Haiger. Mine was the last stop. By the time I got on the little bus all the seats had been taken up and I, along with some kids from the stop before mine who went to higher grades, had to stand, stooped over, or crouch for the duration of the trip. But it wasn't far and the vehicle was warm and dry, and I always made it to school on time. Of course there were no rules about seat belts or other safety violations in those days.

 I don't remember much about this school since I only attended it for a couple of years. I do remember that I had my first English lessons there, which I liked, and that my French teacher always drew her index finger down her long nose to emphasize the nasal sounds of that language, which I did not like. I could simply not comprehend French. I also recall that our geography instructor, Herr Georg, used the same method of punishment that Fräulein Ströhmann and my father used, but only on the girls. I think they all knew each other from teachers' meetings and exchanged ideas. Herr Georg, however, punished the boys differently. He picked them up by the short hair at their temples until they stood on tip-toe and had tears in their eyes, which was an embarrassment for them. Boys didn't cry.

Ursula (Winter) Turner

I remember vividly, taking a spill on my bicycle shortly before reaching the school building one summer day (we only had six weeks of vacation and went to school during part of the summer), and skinning my knee which bled profusely. Using a handkerchief I had dipped into the water of the creek that ran directly past the school, I wiped the blood off, not realizing that the creek was extremely polluted. There was no school nurse to consult. I eventually ended up with a bad infection in the wound that bothered me for weeks.

Finally, this school was the place where I learned from a classmate who lived in another town that her neighbor lady, who had new twin babies, had carried them in her legs instead of her stomach. That's why there were two.

My family moved away before I could finish this school.

Sirens

Chapter 17
Traveling to Launsbach after the War

After Papa had been denazified and cleared of all charges of having been a true Nazi, life went pretty much back to normal for our family, at least what they called normal. To me it was like a different kind of life. Mutti no longer had to take care of the bees, which was Papa's job again, or go to the forest for firewood, since Papa had laid in a huge supply when he was working as a woodcutter. All she did now was to take care of ordinary housework which was actually not all that easy in those days when everything had to be done by hand, and it kept her busy enough. And she continued to tend her garden, which always led to canning and making jams and jellies. Papa did help her with the garden, mostly with the digging of the soil and pulling weeds.

The trains had started to run on a schedule by this time, something Germany is famous for today, allowing Mechthild to return to school and attend classes on a regular basis. She left early in the morning and did not return until late afternoon, so we didn't see much of her.

Everything was new to me. I still wasn't quite sure what they meant by normal, but if it included not having to rush for the shelter in the basement all the time and sitting there waiting for the planes to come, or worrying about bombs falling on our head if we didn't take cover, I was all for it. I also liked being able to live in our old apartment again. I especially appreciated the indoor toilet.

Papa was teaching again. And I was going to school as well. Mechthild was, by then, attending housekeeping and cooking school in Wetzlar, about 30 kilometers (19 miles) away. She took the same train she had taken when she had gone to school in Dillenburg but did not get off at that station. Instead she remained on the train until she reached Wetzlar. With all of us, except Mutti, of course, in school, we had our vacations at the same time. Summer vacations in Germany are only about six weeks long, as mentioned above, but we had several two- or three-week breaks throughout the year, and we spent every one of them in Launsbach at the farm of Papa's parents, even the winter ones when there was no work to be done on the farm.

My father with a friend while riding their motorcycles. In the background is the fortress Gleiberg which is only a short distance from Launsbach

Since we didn't own a car we had to take the train to get there. This meant walking to the train station in Haiger while carrying heavy suitcases. We always had to change trains in Wetzlar which generally meant waiting a period of an hour or more before the train we needed that would take us on to Launsbach arrived. With so many railroad tracks and trains having been bombed during the war, train traffic was still being built up and, at first, was sparse because of

Sirens

the scarcity of trains and because some of the rails had not yet been repaired, but at least they were generally on time. The railroad depot in Wetzlar, where we spent the time between trains, had been heavily bombed during the war, and there was only a small part that still had a roof on it. If we went in summer, we just sat on benches in the other part. But during our Christmas vacation trip we waited in the roofed-over area which was usually very crowded, but warm. It also contained a restaurant of sorts.

The trains of that time offered three classes of travel. First class featured plush seats. Second class had vinyl-covered seats. And in third class you had to make do with wooden benches. Papa saw no sense in spending extra money for comfort when the car's wooden seats would take us to the same destination for less, so we always traveled third class. Some of the third class cars had been converted from cattle cars and had benches only around the walls. Travelers who couldn't find a seat because of the car being crowded had to stand in the large central area and hold onto one of the many straps that hung from the ceiling. If we rode in one of these cars, I usually made room for an adult and sat on one of our suitcases.

Papa and Mutti were thrifty, saving where and when they could. Mutti always packed a lunch for our journey, consisting of hearty rye bread sandwiches and homemade juice. Papa refused to eat at the station restaurant in Wetzlar during our long wait. He always complained, "They should be ashamed of themselves. They are taking advantage of the train travelers by keeping their prices much too high." There was no other eating place in the vicinity, so I guess they did take advantage.

My parents did try to save because they wanted to build a house of their own some day. They never threw anything away before the item had seen its full use. Nothing was wasted. I can still visualize Papa as he read his mail and, when finished, turn each sheet of paper over to see if anything was written on the reverse side. If it was blank, he cut it up into small squares to be used for taking notes or making lists, or writing short messages. He had a whole stack of these in his desk drawer. Had "sticky notes" existed in those days Papa would not have spent money on them.

While Papa saved paper and picked up nails he found lying in the street, straightening the bent ones with his hammer, to be used again, my mother washed the inside of plastic bags she had used, along with the dishes, and used them again.

My father took his shoes to the shoemaker more than once to be resoled, to have the heels straightened, or a seam mended. I often went along because I found the man fascinating and gross at the same time. He was able to turn his eyelids inside-out. He was Elisabeth's uncle.

*   *   *

I loved to sit by the window while traveling by train and I always asked Papa to push it open so I could stick my head out and feel the wind in my face. The train cars got pretty hot in summer. Mutti always held on to my skirt or dress to keep me from falling out. She also cautioned me not to look toward the front because I might get a cinder in my eye. Of course I didn't listen and Mutti had to spit on her hanky and try to get cinders out of my eyes more than once. I always pulled my head back when we went over a bridge because I just knew our train would fall into the river below. I have no idea why I thought pulling my head back would help. I suppose I just didn't want to see it happen when we went head over heels into the water.

Arriving at my grandparents' house, I was always a little worried because I never got over being afraid of Winter Opa even when Papa, who was his son, was there with us, and I know Mechthild felt the same way, although she was older. It was obvious that Opa didn't like kids, in spite of the fact that he had raised four of his own – or perhaps Winter Oma had done most of the raising. He never acted friendly toward us, including our cousins. He growled at us or gave us mean looks. I always hoped he was out in the fields when we got there so I wouldn't have to greet him right away, but that would have just put off the inevitable. If he was at the house, I stayed as far away from him as I possibly could. He generally had a scowl on his face and I don't think I ever saw him smile. The bushy, gray mustache that covered his upper lip didn't help either. It made him look fierce and even meaner. But he never actually hurt any of us kids.

    Winter Oma, who always seemed somewhat aloof (she wasn't raised locally but came from the southern part of Germany), wasn't much better than her husband, although I don't think she disliked kids. She didn't seem to know how to act around us, however, or how to talk to us. She'd give my cousin 50 Pfennig to spend, then turned around and gave me 20 Pfennig. When I asked her why Renate got so much more, she gave me 50 Pfennig, too, but let me keep the 20, and called it even. She did have one quality that endeared her to me – she was a superb cook, although she still put some strange meals on the table, even though the war was now over and food was more plentiful. She didn't usually have to go to the fields because she did the cooking for everyone who had come to help with the work there, which included my two uncles and their wives and kids, besides our small family, and of course, my aunt, Got, and her son, Wolfgang, who lived with them. I would have enjoyed Oma's meals a lot more had I not been made to sit near Opa who looked very unappetizing and could spoil any meal because of the food he always got stuck all over his mustache. Egg yolk was the worst.

Ursula (Winter) Turner

Winter Opa knocks mortar from bricks he has bought from owners of bomb-damaged houses

With Opa's fields located all around the countryside, it took a long time to get from the house to any of them with the cow-drawn wagon, and this left little time to get any of the work done, so he was always glad to get Papa's and my uncles' help. Onkel Emil lived less than 3 kilometers (1 ¾ mile) away in the next town on the other side of the hill. Usually only his daughter, my cousin Renate, accompanied him. His wife, Tante Anneliese was too hoity-toity to get her hands dirty doing farm work. Onkel Reinhold lived in Cologne and he and my aunt Maria and my cousin Friedhelm had to travel even farther than we did, also by train. Since he didn't get the vacations my father and Uncle Emil did, both being teachers, he and his family didn't come as often. Papa's only sister, Got, lived with her parents and was always there to help. She was the official cow-milker. Got had lost both her husband and her older son in the war. I had never met them.

Papa and Winter Oma walk next to the wagon. Oma did help occasionally in the fields. Her house is visible behind them

    Winter Opa grew potatoes, turnips, rye, wheat and oats, and also had a hay meadow for the cows. All the farming was done in a primitive way in the Germany of the 40s and 50s, without the help of any kind of machinery except for the communal thrashing machine. All of the harvest was transported from the fields to the barn by using a wagon which was pulled by the two cows that also served as dairy cows. They were milked by Got every morning before they were hitched to the wagon and every evening after they returned. I loved to watch as the white streams of milk squirted into the bucket that my aunt held between her knees.

    Got was actually Mechthild's godmother. Since my sister was the oldest of her nieces and nephews, we all heard Mechthild call her Got as we came along, so we followed suit and called her the same. The name stuck and even some people from town called her that.

From left: Mechthild, Mutti, Tante Maria, and Got are cutting rye and are getting ready to shock it.

She always sat on her three-legged little stool, her head, covered with a kerchief on, tucked into the cow's side, and the bucket clenched between her knees. She then gently pulled on and stripped the cow's teats until the milk came out. Often the cow would try to switch the flies that were buzzing around its eyes away with its tail while Got was milking. I liked to hold onto the tail to keep it from hitting my aunt in the head. Got let me try to milk a couple of times, but I could never get anything to come out.

I often watched Winter Oma churn butter from the cream that came off the top of the milk. She had an old-fashioned wooden churn with a stick protruding from the center of the lid which she plunged up and down and up and down until, suddenly, there was the butter, all done and ready to eat. It was hard work, and the few times I tried churning butter, my arms ached for a long time afterward.

I didn't mind the hind end of the cows so much. It was the other end that worried me. Since I was just a child, I wasn't expected to do any hard farm work like the adults, and even Mechthild, had to do. But I was given a job. It consisted of my watching the cows, still hitched to the wagon that stood alongside the field on a grassy lane. While the others dug up the potatoes or the turnips with their hoes, I was made to stand in front of the cows, and was told to keep them from wandering off while trying to go after the grass they liked. There I stood, facing those two huge animals, whip in hand – and scared to death. Little did those grown-ups know that, had those cows taken a notion to move on, I sure wasn't going to stand in their way.

One thing I did like about farming was making hay or, to be more precise, my part in it. Everybody helped. The men cut the grass with their big scythes in smooth, long, even strokes, laying it out in rows as they cut it so it could dry in the sun. Later the women used wooden rakes to turn it over and give more of the grass a chance to be exposed to the sun. Finally it was raked into small piles and left to dry some more; and then came the fun part as far as I was concerned. The ladder sides were attached to the wagon to make it taller and allow it to hold a bigger load, and the cows then pulled it to the meadow. With me, and sometimes also Renate on board, the men threw the loose hay over the side of the wagon with their four-pronged pitch forks. Renate's and my job consisted of stomping the hay down as hard as we could to compact it and make as much as possible fit into the wagon. Usually the hay of the entire meadow was hauled in one wagon load. Sometimes we got scratched by the dry heavy stalks of some weed, or the hay would get inside our shoes and socks, but we kept on going until the job was finished. By the time we were done, the wagon was loaded up so high we couldn't climb down by ourselves – and we really didn't want to. The real fun consisted of riding, perched high on top of the wagon, all the way into town and up to the house. There we had to slide down the hay in back of the wagon into the arms of one of the men.

Haying was quite an undertaking in the 1940s and '50s in Germany

    Another part of farm life I liked was to help my aunt feed the animals, keeping my distance from the front of those cows, however. There were also a couple of pigs, a few geese and ducks, and quite a few chickens. I loved gathering the eggs. Even if they were not colored except that some of them were brown instead of white, it was like Easter all over again.

    The worst part for me about our visits to the farm was the inevitable outhouse. In years to come, whenever I visited my relatives in Launsbach, I was always reminded of the Webers. These outhouses, at both of my grandparents' homes, were pretty much the same as the one where the door had to be demolished because of a spider. Since all the buildings at the farm were connected, the outhouse at my paternal grandparents' house was wedged between a shed and the manure pile. A number of bugs and spiders and squirmy things made their home there. It never took me long to do my business.

* * *

Launsbach had a community Backhaus (baking house) where women brought their cakes and their sourdough bread to be baked.

It was not unusual to see farm women on their weekly trek to the Backhaus (I think it was on Fridays), one large cake pan under each arm and another perched on a specially made cushion on top of their head. The Backhaus had two oven doors to allow for better access, but both led to the same huge oven. In the back of this oven branches were set on fire to help it obtain the required baking temperature (I think there were gauges at the oven door to keep track of this). More branches were added as needed by pushing them to the back, past the cakes already baking.

A long table on each side of the room allowed the women to have a place for their cakes while they were waiting their turn. The cakes were placed into the oven by means of a long pole that had a square, flat board nailed to the end of it on which to place the cakes. This was then pushed into the oven where a quick jerk would remove the cake from the board. It seemed like a hard way to do baking, but most of the women from town took part in this once-a-week activity. Of course, they baked their fancier cakes in their ovens at home, which was still not easy since they were part of their wood-burning stoves.

Ursula (Winter) Turner

The old Backhaus (baking house) is only used on special occasions now. A hometown museum is located upstairs

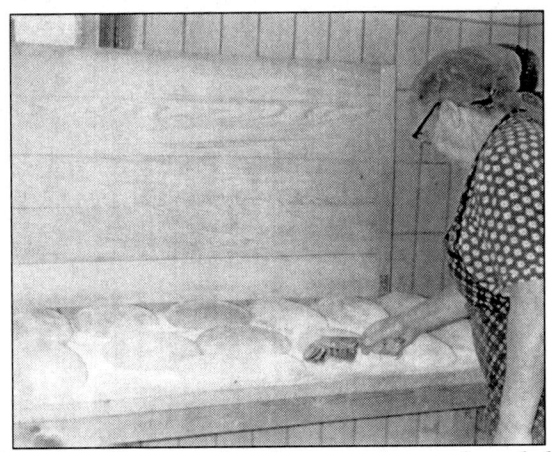

Got brushes flour on her loaves of sourdough bread before they go into the large oven of the Backhaus

Sirens

My aunt participated in this communal baking event every week. She was as good at baking as her mother was at cooking. Her cakes, always made with yeast dough, were delicious, and she always baked several loaves of sourdough bread.

Today, a few women still bake in the Backhaus on special occasions, usually for hometown demonstrations, but also to keep the tradition alive. The second floor of the building houses a small museum

Inside the Backhaus

Ursula (Winter) Turner

Chapter 18
The Butcher Comes to the House

Once a year when it was cold, usually in early January, the two current residents of the pig pen were butchered, with my two uncles splitting one, and my grandparents and Got, and my family dividing the other one between us. This was the pay for all the hard work everybody had done on the farm. Of course we also got to take some of the other products of the farm home, such as potatoes and some plums and apples from the fruit trees.

A man in town, who was a professional butcher and usually worked in a butcher shop, made his rounds of the farms in winter to do the butchering right there on the premises, with all the adults of the household helping.

My cousins and I were not allowed to watch as the pigs were killed. That was considered something too violent for our young eyes to see. After the animals were dead, they were hung by their hind legs on a special contraption the butcher had brought along. Their stomachs were slit open, and then they were left hanging for a while to bleed out. The blood was preserved to make a sort of lunchmeat called, logically, *Blutwurst* (bloodwurst) from it and other ingredients. The butcher took the intestines out of the hogs, emptied them onto the manure pile, cleaned them thoroughly and set them aside to be used for sausage casings.

In the meantime my uncles, Papa and Opa had poured hot water over the still hanging pigs to loosen the bristles. Following this, they used a special tool to scrape their skin to remove them. Finally cold water was poured over the animals.

The women had filled the freshly cleaned, large copper kettle in the summer kitchen that was normally used for doing the laundry, with water and had lit a fire in the fire hole at the bottom.

Eventually the summer kitchen became so crowded with people working, that we children were chased outside and told to play. The butcher had already cut up some meat and mixed some of it to be used for sausage and lunchmeat which was stuffed into large bladders. Some of these, along with some special cuts of meat, were placed into the kettle to cook for a while to preserve the meat and make it last for a longer period of time since refrigeration was not yet available to most homes. The kind of sausage called Bratwurst was Oma's department and she was an expert at it. She mixed ground meat and herbs and spices and then pressed the meat into the cleaned intestines with a tool that could be vaguely compared to a meat grinder, a machine that had also been provided by the butcher. Oma gave the sausage lengths a quick twist whenever each was the length a Bratwurst should be. Eventually a long row of these connected little sausages would rest in front of her on the long table she was using. On the few occasions that I managed to slip in to watch, my mouth always watered at the sight of all this meat. The summer kitchen continued to bustle with activity, with the men cutting up meat into specific pieces such as ribs, or pork chops or roasts, and the women watching the kettle and mixing meat to be canned. I was soon chased outside again to join my cousins who also kept trying to sneak in for a peek at all the activities. Winter Opa was the overseer of the butchering operation and made sure everything ran as smoothly as possible, so we sure didn't want him to catch us.

The butcher always took some of the meat with him to be smoked, since my grandparents did not have a smokehouse. Besides that and the canned meat there was also some that was placed in brine.

I never saw how the rest of the meat, the pieces that were not made into lunchmeat or sausages, such as the pork chops or roasts, were cut up because the adults made doubly sure that we children were not anywhere in the vicinity of the work, some of which took place outdoors for lack of space in the summer kitchen. This time it was not the violence that made the adults keep us away, but the fact that the men were wielding hatchets and sharp knives and didn't have time to watch out for us and keep us from getting hurt as they finished the day's work on temporary plank tables. By the time I was old enough to have been permitted a closer look, both of my grandparents had died and the farm had been sold.

The process of butchering generally took an entire day and involved a lot of work for the adults, while it was filled with excitement for us children. We didn't mind the freezing cold outside, but if we got too chilled, we'd go inside to warm up. We always chose the living room in which to spend our time indoors and continued watching the activities taking place in the yard by pressing our noses against the window panes from which we had an excellent view.

At the end of the day, when their labor was completed, the fun began, even for the adults. We all participated in eating something called *Metzelsuppe* (loosely translated, soup made from pieces) for supper. This was made from the broth in the big kettle which was rich from the meat that had come out of some of the sausage bladders that had burst, something that invariably happened, leaving the contents in the water, along with some smaller pieces of the other meat that had been added to the water later, making for a pretty tasty soup after some rice had been added – and there was always lots of it. Add to this large slices of Got's sourdough bread slathered with Oma's freshly churned butter and some of the day's lunchmeat, and we had a hearty meal. All the neighbors were invited to this feast. The kids all received a small sausage which they were allowed to eat without bread something that was usually not permitted because it was considered wasteful.

The war was over and life was good again.

The odd thing was that the butcher would never join us in this meal since he hated meat, which that was understandable since he was around it so much. Winter Oma knew this and always offered him a cake she had baked earlier especially for him. He never ate any of it on the premises, but took it home with him after his work was finished, to share with his family.

*   *   *

When the end of our visit to the farm approached, I always had mixed feelings about leaving. I liked some of the stuff I got to do on the farm, but I was also looking forward to going home and seeing my friends again. Since Mechthild always had to work so hard on the farm, she couldn't have been happier to be returning home. School was preferable to farm work as far as she was concerned.

And I did hear Mutti mutter on a couple of occasions, "It sure would be nice to be going on a real vacation just once instead of always having to help on the farm." (After their retirement, my parents traveled extensively, taking at least two trips a year as long as they were able.)

Ursula (Winter) Turner

Chapter 19
I Spend Time with the Other Side of the Family

Although we spent a lot of our vacation time at the farm, I did get to go visit Mutti's side of the family, too. Mutti's sister, Tante Gertrud, who had lost her husband in the war, lived on the second floor of the old farmhouse, along with her three sons and Lenchen Oma. The farmland and the barn had been leased to another farm family who lived downstairs in the same house.

I always enjoyed visiting this side of my family because of my cousins who kept me entertained. Dieter was too old for me to play with. He was nearer Mechthild's age. But Jürgen was a year older than I, and Gunter was a year younger. We were like "The Three Musketeers" when we were together and we always created mischief. I even tried to pee like the boys did, standing at the manure pile and using a straw I'd gotten from the barn, but it didn't work. I had to use that darn outhouse. Even at Lenchen Oma's I couldn't get away from that.

Sometimes the three of us walked to the edge of town where the dump was located. We weren't supposed to go there, but we always succeeded in talking each other into going anyway. After all, we managed to find such neat things at the dump, such as partially empty cans of paint that might come in handy sometime, and, once, the skeleton of what might have been a cat. Not being much of a cat lover, it did not affect me as much at that of the dog's I had seen at home. Besides, I had seen the dog when he still had all his fur.

On one particular afternoon – I was probably eight years old – we left the house after Tante Gertrud

Sirens

told us to be home in time for supper, which was served promptly at 6 o'clock. There were so

Lenchen Oma with her grandchildren. She is holding Gunter, Mechthild is standing at her side. I'm in front in my usual pose, then Jürgen and Dieter

many treasures to be investigated at our favorite place that day that we did not pay any attention to the time. When Jürgen, who as the oldest was the only one with a watch, finally looked at it, he let out a little squeak. We were dangerously close to being late, and we knew if we didn't get to the house on time we would be punished by not getting any supper. He quickly suggested we take a shortcut by walking along the railroad tracks – something we were definitely forbidden to do. We didn't have time to debate which would be worse, being late or being discovered on the tracks. We decided to take a chance on not being seen among the dense foliage that grew on both sides of the tracks.

Everything was going well, and we made good progress until we heard a whistle in the distance, after which we made even better time. A train was approaching but we couldn't get off the tracks because we were in the center of a long overpass with no place to go. We ran as fast as our feet would carry us, hoping not to trip over any of the railroad ties. Just as the train came into view around a curve, we got to the end of the overpass and managed to get onto the road that crossed the tracks at this point. Panting from our exertions, we looked at each other, grinned, and continued toward my cousins' home, reaching it just in time for the meal. I don't believe we walked along the tracks again although, as far as I know, nobody ever found out about our near disaster which was surprising since most of the trains that ran along that track were passenger trains and it would have been easy for somebody on the train to spot us through the window. I don't remember if we paid any more visits to the dump. We probably did, but we found other exploits to occupy our time as well.

We were always in search of money which we wanted to use to buy candy. But money was hard to come by at our age. Our allowances were not large, and that was about the only income we had, unless we received some cash for our birthdays.

One day we came up with the idea of selling some of our treasured possessions. We went to our hiding place in the barn and carried out the almost empty cans of paint we had found at the dump, as well as some old wire and some empty tin cans. The boys contributed some of their old and broken toys and I added a few pretty rocks I had found. Then I went to the back yard and picked a few wild flowers that grew along the fence and put them in the tin cans along with some water. We set up in front of the gate to the yard by placing a board across some bricks and displaying our wares on the board. Sadly, not one single person of the ones who walked by, and there were quite a few since few people drove, showed an interest in what we had for sale. The flowers wilted and we finally gave up, not a *Pfennig* richer.

The three of us often used bikes as our way to get around town. There was an extra bike Dieter had outgrown that Tante Gertrud had kept for my use. We always took the lower street to cross the village because my other grandparents lived on the upper street and I didn't want to go past their house in case I was seen by somebody there and would be asked to do some kind of minor chore, which would definitely spoil our fun.

Daring as my cousins were, they often rode their bikes without placing their hands on the handlebars. Not to be outdone, I soon learned to do this little trick and followed suit in spite of the roughness of the street. We didn't know at the time that this was against the law, but one day we found out. As we traveled along the main street, our usual route, one day, not using our hands as had become our habit, although it was difficult to do on the bumpy cobblestones, we got caught. A policeman who'd been driving through town from our larger neighboring town toward Gießen (Launsbach didn't rate a police station either, just like Allendorf, because of its small size), followed us when he saw what we were doing. Suddenly he passed us, stopping his car in front of us and, getting out of it, held up his hand. We knew immediately that we were in trouble. The policeman didn't hesitate one minute, but gave us a severe tongue lashing, pointing out the dangers that could befall us when not holding onto the handlebars – the accidents we might cause to ourselves as well as others as a consequence of losing control of our bicycles if, by chance, we hit a small rock or a pot hole. And he threatened to notify our parents if he ever caught us riding our bikes in that fashion again. I would like to be able to say that he taught us a lesson, but I remember riding my bicycle, even at home, without using my hands, whenever the chance presented itself, always keeping an eye out for policemen, though. It didn't occur to me until much later that the policeman who had stopped us had not asked us our names, so how would he have known which parents to notify.

There were two events I especially looked forward to on our visits to Launsbach. These were the circus and the carnival that both came to Gießen during the summer, but at different times. Haiger featured an annual carnival, but it was small and dinky compared to the one in Gießen. The circus came to that town only rarely.

We usually walked to Gießen when we wanted to take in these events. None of the adults wanted to spend money on bus fare for so many people, and nobody owned a car at this time. Usually my parents came along as did Lenchen Oma and Tante Gertrud and, of course, Jürgen, Gunter and I. Mechthild was doing her apprentice work by then and did not often come with us on vacation.

As we entered the outskirts of town, it soon became evident how much destruction this city had suffered from the air-raids. Ruins of bombed houses lined both sides of the street with some of them

Sirens

consisting only of an outer, burned out shell of bricks. Some had small trees and bushes growing inside that were visible through gaping window holes. Others had been reduced to nothing but a pile of rubble that had not yet been cleared away. The downtown area was evidently being restored first since a few new buildings had already been erected, but work was ongoing to rebuild the entire city, putting things back as close as possible to the way it had been – a daunting task that would require a lot of materials, labor and time.

As we walked toward the site of the circus which was thankfully located on the side of town that was closer to Launsbach keeping us from having to walk quite so far, there was still so much damage, so much devastation visible. We all looked around, taking in the destruction that had been done to Gießen during the war. Oma guessed it would take years to have all the rubble removed and new houses built in place of the old ones that had been destroyed by the bombs. Just as she was saying that, I spotted a house that no longer had a front, but a bathtub was still hanging onto a side wall on what would have been the second floor – only there was no longer a floor. Some greenery was growing in the tub and was hanging over its side.

The school I attended later on after we moved to Launsbach had received a direct hit on one wing bringing with it a lack of classroom space and, although school in Germany is generally held only in the mornings, we had to attend one afternoon a week until that side of the building had been restored.

*   *   *

The circus always had only one big ring which, in my opinion, makes more sense, because you always miss seeing some of the action in a three-ring circus. My favorite, as with most kids, were the clowns. But I was always awed by the big animals, the elephants the lions and tigers, as well as the trapeze artists. We had a big swing in our attic at home and I was later tempted to try some of the latter's tricks, but I couldn't get any of my friends to go along with my plan.

While we had to sit still at the circus and follow the action, the carnival gave us a chance to use up some of our own energy as we went on the various rides and became more and more daring as we got older. There were also stands where you could win things. People were offered little rolls of paper for 10 Pfennig each and when you unrolled them, a printed message inside would tell you what you had won. If you were unlucky, which was most of the time, it would say *Niete* which was the carnival's way of saying: "Try again." However, the items that could be won were often useful. I mainly remember glass dishes of various sizes. I also remember stuffed animals, small ones and large ones.

On one of my visits to Lenchen Oma's house – this was during Christmas vacation when I was about to turn ten – I got there just after my cousins had returned from a visit to a neighbor's house. Loud voices could be heard as I approached the open door to the kitchen. The boys were standing in front of their mother and, to my amazement and delight, Gunter was holding a cute and wiggly little *Dackel* (dachshund) puppy under his arm. My cousin's voice was raised until it almost squeaked and he was pleading with his mother to let them keep the little dog. "They don't want him!" he told her near tears, "They'll kill him if they don't find somebody to take him!" Jürgen stood by not saying anything, but the look on his face told the story. He, too, wanted their mother to let them keep the little dog.

My aunt sounded pretty much like my parents had when I'd asked for a dog of my own. She answered with a firm "No." It seemed as though she had already explained to them why their household could not afford the added burden of a dog.

Sirens

I had wanted a dog as long as I could remember. My parents had always stood firm, giving as their most compelling reason for their denial of my wish that we lived upstairs and it would be too difficult to housebreak a dog, as well as to walk him every day.

When they joined us later at Oma's house I immediately told them about the puppy. Gunter had been allowed to keep him until I received my parents' verdict, after I had told Tante Gertrud that I was going to ask them if I could have the puppy. I instructed Gunter immediately after they arrived to go get the puppy from his temporary bed, hoping that if Mutti and Papa could see how cute the little dog was, it would influence their decision. I also used the same persuasion Gunter had used, even though it hadn't worked for him, nevertheless hoping it would do the trick for me. "He's so cute," I pointed out. "Just look at those droopy ears and that little tail and those short legs. And they are going to kill him if they can't find a home for him." I also promised to feed him, walk him, and clean up any messes he might make.

On our way back to Allendorf, the train had an extra passenger. I had finally gotten my wish. I was now the proud owner of my own pet, a little dog I named Lumpi (pronounced Loompy). On the train trip I kept the puppy in a zippered canvas tote bag, zipping it up to where only his head stuck out. We weren't sure if dogs were allowed in passenger compartments, but we certainly weren't going to make the little thing travel in the cold baggage car. So, whenever the conductor approached, I poked Lumpi's head gently into the bag and zipped it all the way up, hiding my little dog from the man just in case.

When we arrived in Haiger it was dark and cold, and we still faced that long walk home. I decided that Lumpi would be too cold in his canvas bag, so I buttoned him into the front of my heavy, wool coat with, again, only his head sticking out. And, although he got a bit heavy after a while, I continued carrying him under my coat and we kept each other warm in this fashion.

Lumpi ended up being as much Mutti's dog as he was mine as she had probably foreseen when denying my request for a dog all those times before. But I knew she liked him as much as I did. Since I was in school for a big part of the day, I couldn't always do the chores as I'd promised, so Mutti took care of Lumpi when I couldn't and I believe the two of them grew very close during my absences.

My very first dog, Lumpi

I was nineteen years old when I left for America, and Lumpi was nine. A number of friends and family members had stopped by the house to see me off, and in all the commotion and excitement I didn't get to say good bye to little Lumpi. I never saw him again. By the time I was able to return to Germany for a visit, my little dog had died. But I thank my cousin Gunter for bringing him into my life. We had a lot of fun

Chapter 20
Toys and Activities in the Post-War Years

Thinking back now, there were many wonderful moments throughout my childhood, in spite of the fact that I spent the first part of it in an ongoing war. Until 1945, the children of my generation had never experienced peace. But we didn't miss what we had never had and knew nothing about.

Most of the good times naturally took place after the war was over, and I felt as though I was just then starting to live. Despite my tender years, the depression and fear of the adults around me must have transferred themselves onto me, and when the horror was over, it felt as though something heavy had been lifted off me. There were no more sirens in the night nor were there any of the accompanying hurried trips to the dark basement filled with worried looking grown-ups and sleepy children. Mutti laughed more often, and Papa was home again. Most of the adults around us were more cheerful, with the exception of those who had lost loved ones in the war. Some of these people, mostly women, still looked and acted somber. They continued to wait and hope that their husbands, sons or brothers would return home some day, never having received word that their men were dead, only that they had been declared as missing. Got was one of them. The last time she had heard from either her husband or son was when they had been fighting in Russia. Since that time there had been no sign of life from either one. They were missing, but neither my uncle nor my cousin ever came home again. Some of those loved ones did return – sometimes months or even years later – often lacking an arm or a leg or both, having lost them during the fighting. It was not unusual to see these wounded warriors dressed in rags and sitting on blankets alongside buildings in big cities, begging for handouts. When I first saw them I always stared because I felt sorry for them and I wanted to give them something. But Mutti pointed out that they were getting money from the state and many had perfectly good homes and nice families to go to and that they were just doing this to get more money and because they couldn't do anything else due to their injuries.

Still, none of it affected me as much as it might have had I been a little older when the war started. I didn't know any of my family members who had died in the war because they had all left for the fighting before I was born. I felt sorry for Tante Gertrud and Got, and when I looked at the picture of my cousin, Heinz that was hanging on Got's living room wall, I wished I could have met him before he had died. He had been a handsome young man. However, both of my aunts seemed to be holding up fairly well and continued with their lives as best they could, so I didn't concern myself too much. Tante Gertrud remarried after a while and had another son. Got and her younger son, Wolfgang, continued living with our grandparents. She remained a widow until her own death.

I did know one man personally who had lost a leg, but he didn't sit on a street corner with a cup for change in his hand. Herr Pfeiffer had served with Papa during the war and since the Pfeiffers only lived three towns away from us with the distances between towns never very far in Germany (Mutti had visited Frau Pfeiffer several times by bicycle during the war) we used to pay frequent visits to them. Even after the war many people still traveled by bicycle. With most bus traffic not having started yet, it was difficult for Herr Pfeiffer to visit us since he couldn't use the pedals on a bike very well with only one leg, so we usually visited them. The Pfeiffers owned a small neighborhood grocery store, and I never left there without a chocolate bar in my pocket.

Sirens

When at home, I was always ready to go outside and play and forget about the war and the bombs. Those memories soon faded from my mind and were only occasionally and dimly thought of. Despite the freedom I now had, I was often dissatisfied and sometimes considered my days boring. There simply wasn't a whole lot to do for children of that time. There was still a scarcity of toys. We certainly didn't have the variety and choices that today's children enjoy.

I can't count the times when I ran up to Mutti and complained of having nothing to do. Mechthild was always away at school and later, at work, when she no longer lived with us. Heidi often had to accompany her mother on errands. Elsa liked to help her dad in their garden. And sometimes even I got tired of reading. We did have a number of simple toys and games that could have occupied my time, but the problem was that most of these required more than one person to play. Mechthild would have been too old to play a lot of them anyway, even if she had been home. With no other siblings, I had nobody to play with when my friends were otherwise occupied. To compound my problem, many of the village's children would not come to our apartment, especially after Papa became principal of the school, because it would have meant coming to the principal's home, a man they respected almost to the point of fear. Although Papa was never mean to any of his students, they kept their distance because, besides the mayor and the preacher, the principal was one of the most important people in town.

Bored or not, at this time of my life I didn't have a worry in the world – with the exception of making good grades in school. Being young, I knew I was invincible and felt that I was able to do anything I set my mind to, without limits, as did most of my friends. As a child, your dreams are still new and alive, and the possibilities of the future are endless. The war was in the past. The adults had surely learned their lessons

Ursula (Winter) Turner

and, after all the gruesome years of the war, there couldn't possibly be another one. The sirens had been stilled.

So I went on with my life and spent time with my friends whenever I could and stopped flinching when I heard a plane flying in the sky above.

I spent most of my playtime with my best friend Heidi, who was only three months younger than I. Sometimes we were joined by Elisabeth from down the street, who was a grade above us, her cousin Thea who lived in the same house as Elisabeth and was in our grade, or Elsa from across the street who was a grade below us. Rosel made up the rest of the group when she was home on vacation from deaf school. She was two months younger than I.

Heidi and I didn't let the lack of toys interfere with our fun. When it came to playing, we sometimes dreamed up the weirdest things. One year, when we were still attending grade school we had both received small metal scoops and buckets for Easter to be used in a sand box. The problem was – we didn't have a sandbox. So we came up with something useful we could do with our scoops. We had heard that China was on the other side of the earth from us, which made us reason that, if we were on the top, the Chinese had to be at the bottom. We didn't give it much thought how they stayed there without falling off, but made up our minds to dig a hole so deep that we would come out in China so we could see for ourselves what it was like to live on the bottom of the earth. I'm sure many other children have thought of this, but we were very serious about it.

The digging kept us occupied for the bigger part of an afternoon after school was out and we'd done our homework, until Mutti called for me from the kitchen window to come in for supper. "I can't come in yet!" I hollered back. "We haven't made it through to China yet!" She didn't laugh, but she did inform us with a straight face that it was impossible for us to do so

Sirens

because we didn't have the right equipment. What did she think our scoops were for?

We dug again the next day but hit rock and decided right then we didn't want to go to China after all because we didn't speak their language.

Some days we spent making little dolls from fabric, cotton balls and sticks. We made some into Indians and some into Cowboys and played with them under a bush in the front yard. We were always on the side of the Indians because we felt they had been treated badly. We didn't know about the soldiers then and had the cowboys fight against them.

Heidi was probably the only one of my friends who wasn't afraid to come to our apartment, so, since we had more room, we spent time there when the weather was bad.

One rainy day we decided to do some coloring. Sitting at the small table by the kitchen window where I usually did my homework, we drew pictures of flowers, animals and people and colored them in with my coloring pencils of which I owned a cigar box full in many different colors and lengths. Then we cut out the pictures separately into little squares. The next day the sun was shining again. We took our "beautiful" paintings and, with the idea of making people happy, placed our works of art into mailboxes throughout the neighborhood. We were sorry we couldn't see the people's smiling faces when they discovered our gifts. Most of the lucky recipients probably wondered where their strange mail came from. Some might have guessed. We never told anyone about what we had done, not even our parents.

The school building was a paradise for us children on rainy days. It was so large that it became our indoor playground if we didn't feel like pursuing activities that required us to sit still. From the attic, where we had a big swing and large open spaces with plenty of room to play with our dolls, to the basement, where we occasionally got into mischief, to Papa's classroom, in which he sometimes let us play school. The opportunities were endless.

Heidi's mother regularly brewed her own beer which she stored in their part of the basement. One day we decided to see what the big deal was all about that made adults drink this stuff and made them forbid us children to touch it. "If we open a bottle, we have to drink it all," warned Heidi, "because then we can put it with the empty bottles and my mother will never know the difference. But if we just drink a little, Mamma will notice and I'm sure she'll suspect us." It never occurred to us that we could have poured out what we didn't want, although it might have been dangerous for us to be caught carrying a bottle to the sink in the laundry room.

At any rate, the stuff tasted awful. But we sat in the dark corner where the beer was kept and bravely passed the bottle back and forth until it was empty. Mutti never did figure out why I seemed kind of wobbly that evening and she couldn't get over the fact that I volunteered to go to bed before my bedtime. She felt my forehead, and although she didn't detect any signs of a fever she still assumed that I might be coming down with a cold again and took my temperature to be on the safe side. Of course, it was normal, but she was, nevertheless, glad when I felt all right the next morning.

One of our favorite activities in the basement took place shortly after Christmas each year. Since my parents always kept their Christmas tree up until my birthday in early January, Heidi begged her mother to give us theirs. We lugged it down from their third floor room to the laundry room which had a concrete floor and walls, and not much else on one side of it, scattering dry needles along the entire route down the stairs without bothering to clean them up, for which we got into trouble. We were made to pick up every single needle.

We set the tree in a corner and decorated it with handmade ornaments, adding candle stubs we had been given by both of our mothers. Since we had no clip-on candle holders, we fastened the candles to the tree branches with straight pins that we pushed through the branches first and then through the bottoms of the candles. We were just as careful as our mothers in placing the candles by making sure there wasn't a branch above any of the candles. After we had lit them, we sat on an old wooden bench and watched as the candle flames flickered in our tree. Nobody on either side of our families seemed concerned about our activities in the basement. I guess, since we had made it through a dangerous war, our parents were not overly protective of us at that time. Besides, we did try to be careful and nothing ever happened. However, had the tree actually caught fire, there was nothing in that corner that could burn, and the water hose that was used to fill the laundry kettle was nearby.

An old man from the village was the school's janitor. His main duty consisted of keeping the boiler in the basement that heated all the classrooms, going during wintertime. He also swept and scrubbed the classrooms and the big central hall and picked up trash from the schoolyard. We visited him sometimes when he was in the basement and often wondered why he kept smelling the base of his thumb and then sneezed shortly after he had done this. When I finally got up the nerve to ask him about this habit of his, he showed us how he, by holding his thumb a certain way, created a small indentation at its base into which he poured some brown stuff that he called snuff. He then showed us how to sniff this, holding first one nostril, then the other shut and inhaling deeply. Then he offered to let us try. Heidi and I were both game, but were caught in such fits of sneezing afterward, although we had not been able to make a large indentation in our small hands, that we never wanted to do this again and could not understand why the janitor would want to. When the old man, whose name I have forgotten, became ill and had to give up the job, Herr Meyer took over, and we didn't care to visit with him.

*   *   *

We turned into regular daredevils when we got our stilts out. Some of the boys in our neighborhood had very tall stilts. Heidi's and mine were much shorter. Protective gear such as helmets or elbow and knee pads was unheard of in those days. If you fell, you ended up with a lump on your head or with scraped knees or elbows. If you were really unlucky, you might even break an arm or a leg.

The school building's wide outside stairs were very tempting for us. Somebody was always daring somebody else to climb the steps while walking on their stilts. Naturally we'd been warned repeatedly by our parents not to do this. But what did they know about what kids were capable of accomplishing? They just wanted to ruin our fun. Going up the steps on stilts sounded exciting and had to be tried.

At first we practiced on a set of lower stairs after which we tried the main stairs, making it up only a few steps before we got scared. But each time we tried, we went a little farther up, until at last we made it all the way to the top. Coming back down was a different story. It was frightening to look down all those steps and I wasn't sure I wanted to do this. The boys attempted it first. I didn't want to follow them, neither did Heidi. We never got the chance to test our courage because one of the boys missed a step and fell halfway down those hard, concrete stairs. He was one of the unlucky ones and broke his leg. After that Heidi and I were not allowed to use our stilts for one entire month.

My parents and her mother discussed it and agreed on this punishment. In addition, we were told to completely stay away from the stairs when using our stilts or face dire consequences. Using the stilts only on level ground seemed quite tame and was no fun at all.

The stairs we used to climb with our stilts

The boy who had broken his leg became our hero, but lost that status as soon as the cast had come off.

We had no organized sports of any kind in either grade school or through the community. The closest I ever came to gymnastics before I turned ten was when a band of gypsies came to town and set up camp. They put on quite a show that evening of bending their bodies as though they had no bones and were made of rubber. One young girl in particular was able to bend her arms and legs every which way. People were glad to pay the small admission fee, even though it meant standing around on the grass while watching the show. We were starved for any kind of entertainment. The gypsies were gone the next day, along with a lot of people's belongings, especially clothes that had been hanging on the line to dry, and a couple of bicycles.

After that experience, a few of the girls tried to make what was called a bridge by standing up, then bending backward and touching their hands to the ground. I was never limber enough to accomplish this, but a few of my friends managed this feat.

Other entertainment consisted of walking up the hill on Sunday afternoons to where the soccer field was located. To get there, we took the same road we had taken to gather up wood. Soccer games took place weekly and the competition was among teams made up of young men of Allendorf and those of neighboring towns. Heidi's younger brother, Ede (his actual name was Eduard), was one of the Allendorf players.

Some of the more macabre happenings to which we sometimes were unintentional witnesses were the numerous traffic accidents that took place on a sharp curve of the highway before it entered town and on another curve halfway through town. This road also had a very steep incline. The accidents occurred regularly, with numerous injuries and quite a few deaths. One incident in particular has stayed in my mind to this day.

A truck had crashed on the upper curve and there had not been enough time yet to remove the wreckage when the very next day a motorcyclist lost control and ran into the remains of the wrecked truck. As fate would have it, the poor man was decapitated by a piece of steel from the earlier wreck. Heidi and I happened upon the scene shortly after it occured and discovered the severed head in a pool of blood.

Eventually 118 people where killed during a ten-year period due to accidents on the two curves. A new road with a gentler incline had been started before the war, with the two bridges already finished at that time, but the construction had to be put on hold at the beginning of the hostilities. The work was back on track in 1946 and the new road was completed in 1950.

The lower of the two death curves in Allendorf. Shown is a truck after it ran into a house. Eventually 118 people lost their lives on this curve and the one above it before a new road was built

I never learned to swim. There was no swimming pool in Allendorf, nor was there one to be found in any of the neighboring towns that were within walking distance, except for Haiger, and for some reason my parents would not let me go there. I think they were afraid I would drown, and they never had time to come along to make sure I was safe. Mutti wouldn't have been of much help anyway because she didn't know how to swim either, nor did Mechthild. Private pools were unheard of. Some of the bigger boys would paddle around in the bigger bomb craters that had filled with rainwater. Other than that, the closest place for a cooling dip on a hot summer day was the creek, the *Haigerbach*, where the water, at its deepest point, was barely deep enough to reach my ten-year-old waist. If you tried to swim, the water soon got shallower until you scraped your knees on the rocks at the bottom. To make matters worse, we were never allowed to go to the creek during any of the many polio scares. But it was a good place to cool off when we were allowed to go there.

Hopscotch was another summer activity that kept us occupied. All we needed was some chalk which Papa was happy to supply, and a small, flat rock. A concrete sidewalk helped, too. Not many of those existed, but we were lucky to have one in front of the school.

Sometimes Heidi and I would spread blankets on the grass of the meadow where Mutti bleached her white clothes, and we sunbathed while looking at the fluffy clouds overhead, discussing the shapes we were seeing in them. Nobody worried about skin cancer then. We had never heard of it.

We also played a game using one of the big, colorful rubber balls we often got for Easter, even after we stopped believing in the Easter bunny. Each one of us took a turn bouncing it against an outside wall, usually the school toilet because home owners complained if we used their house walls. We did the bouncing with different parts of our body: Once with the head; twice with the chest, three times with the inside of the forearm, and so on until we reached ten with the knee or something similar. You lost if you dropped the ball and then it was the next girl's turn. Boys didn't play this. It was considered a sissy game.

Jump ropes were popular as well. There were short ones we could jump by ourselves or long ones that required two other kids, one at each end, who twirled it, while one or two of us jumped.

We didn't have a movie theater in Allendorf, and since the one in Haiger only showed movies at night, I couldn't go because I wasn't allowed outside after dark. Due to the war, not many movies had been made in Germany anyway, so most of these being shown were

Sirens

American movies that had been dubbed into German. Once in a while a movie was shown in the community room of the tavern and that was a really big treat for us.

The radio seldom broadcasted anything for children back then. My parents listened mostly to the news and classical music.

One thing that American kids do in the spring, we always did in the fall – flying kites. With open spaces at a premium, the fields were the only place where we could run far enough to launch a kite, and then only after the crops had been harvested.

I must admit that I never managed to get my kites to go up. Papa built a new one each year from narrow strips of wood and some of the wax paper from the roll that had come from the bombed train. Mutti donated rags from her rag bag for the tail. My father always managed to get my kite to stay way up in the sky after which he let me hold onto the string.

On winter evenings, after we'd had our supper and the dishes had been done, I played with my dolls, colored pictures in my coloring book, or read. Sometimes the four of us, Mutti, Papa, Mechthild, if she was home, and I, got together and played cards or board games. Mechthild didn't finish her education until she was twenty-five years old because so many of the schools she attended were either damaged or had been destroyed in bomb attacks. She also missed many of her school days due to the air-raids. So she was usually home in the evenings. She did work as an intern on two occasions, each time for about half a year, and she had to live at her place of work. The first time she stayed at a private home, the second time in a large home where people went to recuperate from surgery or from long-lasting illnesses. It was her job to do cook special meals for people on a diet.

There was one thing I had been anxious to do that I thought I would love, but I eventually learned to hate it. It was playing the piano. We had an old one that had been sitting in the living room ever since I could remember, but nobody ever used it, and I thought it would be nice to learn how to play this instrument. After I had talked my parents into letting me have lessons, they had it tuned, and I was all set to become a great pianist. It didn't take many lessons before I became greatly disappointed, not in the playing, but in the teacher. I probably would not have hated my lessons had it not been for Herr Reckmann who had taken Herr Löber's place in the classrooms below and who now lived, along with his family, in the Löbers old apartment. Papa, always thrifty, had offered the man some honey in exchange for my lessons. I don't know what kind of a teacher Herr Reckmann was downstairs, but he made my life miserable with his piano teaching methods. He was strict, he was relentless and, worst of all, he was sarcastic when it came to a ten-year-old's attempts to satisfy his demands. He was the one person I did not miss when we moved away. Elsa told me much later that he had been arrested for molesting young boys.

After we moved, I never took another piano lesson. They had left a bad taste in my mouth.

Chapter 21
Outdoor Winter Entertainment

Each winter during those postwar years brought lots and lots of snow. The children in my neighborhood, including me, of course, could hardly wait for those first snowflakes to fall. The cold, rainy days of fall had been boring because we had to stay indoors so much and we were eager to go outside again, especially when it meant being able to play in the snow.

A friend and I are sledding down the entrance way to the school yard. At age 3, I was not yet allowed to go to the roads we sledded down later. Elsa's house can be seen in the background. She still lives there

We lived close to the edge of town in two directions. There was the valley with meadows and the creek at the back of the school building past the schoolyard. And there were only four houses along the street that the school building faced before the open fields started in that direction, fields that had narrow roads between them on which the farmers pulled the

Ursula (Winter) Turner

wagons to take their crops home. These roads weren't much more than paths and were mostly covered with grass, except for two grooves which had been cut, one on each side, by the metal-covered wooden wheels of the farm wagons. The fields were located on a fairly steep slope and came down from the woods that stretched past the village. It was these fields and roads we usually headed for after a good snow because they were ideal for sledding.

After school and lunch for which I could barely sit still, eating very little, Papa brought the sled up from the basement. Although I had left no doubt that I was anxious to get going, Papa would not be hurried. He was always very methodical and did things in his own, thorough way. At the beginning of each sledding season, he rubbed the metal runners carefully with bacon rind that Mutti had provided, while I stood by impatiently. Finally, when he was satisfied he'd covered every inch of metal with grease, he handed the sled over to me. This process took care of whatever rust might have built upon the metal runners through the summer and it made the sled glide so much better. I knew that, but I also knew that my friends were waiting.

With this first snow I was allowed to go sledding right away. After that I had to do my homework first before I was released from the house to have fun. I always hated that because it got dark so early in winter and I had a curfew. I had to be home by dusk.

Mutti always made sure I was dressed in warm clothes. She didn't want to take a chance on my catching one of my many colds, or the tonsillitis from which I suffered throughout my childhood even after the war. She always bundled me up real well before allowing me to escape outside into the cold winter air. We started out with a child's cotton undershirt and matching panties. Then there were the long, woolen stockings that were fastened to a narrow garter belt, worn over the panties. Then came the inevitable dress which most parents of the time decreed girls should wear. I was allowed to wear sweatpants with elastic in the waist and legs under my dress when I went sledding. As I got older, about the time I entered my teens, I actually received permission to leave the dress at home. My outerwear consisted of a padded, hooded jacket and a pair of mittens that were connected by a long string which Mutti had run through the sleeves of the jacket with one mitten poking out of each sleeve. She did this to keep me from losing them. All this was topped with a knitted, wooly cap that tied under my chin. I can remember one style of cap very well due to its name and the way it looked. We called it devil's cap, because it had two points at the crown that looked like little horns and it also came to a point in the center of the forehead. These caps were popular for a long time and many mothers knitted them for their girls.

    By the time Mutti was done with me, I could barely move, but I was made to wear all these clothes when sledding or ice skating. If it was exceptionally cold, I had to wear a cardigan under my jacket.

    Soon Heidi and I were on our way, joined by several other kids, most of them about our age, who were all heading for the open fields with each of us pulling a sled behind us. We didn't have to worry about traffic along the way to the fields because the road we took turned into a narrow farm lane at the last house; few people owned cars anyway. We weren't likely to run into any farmers at this time of year when snow was covering the ground.

    If it had snowed a lot and the snow was deep, the sledding was always slow during the first few trips down the hill before the snow was packed down by repeated runs. We usually started out sitting on our sleds when we sledded down the steep hill, but that soon got boring, so, by the time it was nice and slick, we were zipping down the now slick road head-first, lying on our stomachs. In this position we used the toes of our boots either as brakes, or to hook into the front of the sled behind us, eventually making a long chain and stopping only when we reached the valley floor. What a long way we had to climb to get back to the top.

Before long the snow we'd been scraping with our boots, either the heels or toes, wore off, letting the grass show through. That problem was quickly solved by moving the entire operation to the next road on the other side of the field, and so on, down the line. There were several of these lanes, although each one was less steep than the one before and was, therefore, not as much fun. Each road had to be broken in again, just like the first one to make it smooth and slippery. It was usually time to go home before we made it to the last one.

The older kids, mostly teenagers, used the village streets where the snow was generally packed down a little more. Also, there was asphalt underneath to make the rides smoother and much faster. Even here there wasn't much traffic to worry about and the few drivers who came along knew to watch out for the kids on a snowy day. My friends and I were not allowed by our parents to sled on the streets. Heidi, however, tried it once and promptly ran into a fence because she lost control due to the speed her sled had accumulated, and sprained her middle finger, leaving the joint stiff and swollen from that time on.

My parents were very strict and I had a curfew, which meant I had to be home by dusk. But I always had so much fun sledding with my friends, and since most of them did not have to be home so early, I didn't want to leave either. Who'd want to go home when the other kids were still sledding and were having a ball? Besides, how could I tell if it was dark when the whole world was so white and bright? So, with these possible excuses in my head, I often got home late, ready to use one of them. But none of them worked on my parents. They recognized them for what they were and I, as a result, received my due punishment.

    I never noticed how cold it got when the sun went down until I finally made it home and started thawing out. When I arrived at our apartment, I first received a scolding. Then Mutti made me take off my wet mittens, my jacket, cap and also my boots. She hung the wet clothes on the backs of chairs that she pushed close to the kitchen stove. She stuffed my boots with old newspapers to help them keep their shape and placed them on newspapers on the floor near the stove. Sometimes they were still damp the next morning because the fire was always put out when my parents went to bed, but I only had the one pair, so I had to wear them, which made Mutti worry all the more that I might catch a cold. Not until my boots were off did I realize how cold my toes were and that there were little balls of frozen snow all around my stockings where the tops of my boots had been. It sure felt good to get those stockings off and put my fuzzy house slippers on. By then my ears and feet were beginning to thaw out, too, and, boy, did they hurt when this process was going on. My lips were usually so stiff from the cold when I first came in, I could barely talk to give one of my excuses for my tardiness. At the same time, my nose seemed to be running continuously and Mutti always had to hand me her handkerchief and tell me to blow hard and to quit my sniffling. But none of that bothered me much. I was always ready to go again the next day.

    However, as I mentioned earlier, my tardiness never went unpunished. Once again I had given reason to be grounded and I had to watch through the kitchen window for at least a couple of days as my friends pulled their sleds past the school building on their way to have fun in the snowy fields at the edge of town. And I could only hope that the snow would last long enough for me to be able to enjoy it again after I was allowed to go back outside.

I was never physically punished by Mutti. We were one of those typical "wait till your father comes home" kind of family. Papa sometimes employed Fräulein Ströhmann's method (or perhaps she got it from him since he seemed to have a never-ending supply of thin sticks). He often used one of those sticks to smack the palm of my hand. But the punishment my parents doled out as a rule was to ground me, which meant I had to stay in my room for whatever number of days – or weeks – my parents had decided on. We had no television or telephone, and the only radio was still being kept in the living room. I had books in my room but was not permitted to read them during any given punishment period. Since my parents knew only too well how much I enjoyed reading, they did not consider that a punishment in my case. I was encouraged to do needlecraft which I enjoy now but hated back then. I could not receive friends and could not leave my room except for meals or to use the restroom and, of course, to attend school. I could not even call out to my friends from the windows.

If the punishment was an extra long one, I was allowed to spend time in other parts of the apartment toward the end of it. Depending on the severity of my "crime" I might be grounded for up to four weeks. I would have much rather taken a good whipping just to get it over with. But I'm sure my parents knew this and therefore always punished me with something I hated in order to make me behave the next time so as not to have to endure the grounding again. I can't say that it worked very well.

*   *   *

Each year during the autumn months the creek that flowed along the bottom of the valley ran over its banks, flooding the nearby meadows. Since Allendorf was much too small to offer the children an ice skating rink, nature provided one for us by freezing the water that covered the meadows, creating a somewhat bumpy, wavy, but relatively safe skating rink for us. We usually headed there if there didn't happen to be much snow on the ground.

Mutti and Papa never objected when I asked for permission to go skating. They were strong believers in strenuous, physical, exercise and fresh air. And they knew our skating rink was reasonably safe, with no deep water under the ice. However, I had to promise not to venture out on the creek, even if it was very cold and the top of the water was frozen solid. They also knew I was more likely to come home on time because skating was more tiring than sledding. Besides, we needed daylight to negotiate around the bumps on the ice.

After obtaining permission, Heidi and I slung our skates over our shoulders, made sure we had the keys which we wore on a string around our necks, and headed toward the frozen meadows on the other side of the road where the land was more level. It usually seemed as though all the children of the village were already assembled there.

Ours skates were the kind that had to be screwed to the soles of our boots by means of the key we had taken with us. Turning the key brought the skate clamps closer together until they gripped the soles tightly. We had to sit on the ice to accomplish this procedure. Once we got going, we had lots of accidents due to tripping over uneven places in the ice, or hitting protruding rocks or clumps of grass. This would often cause my boot soles to be ripped off. Papa and I paid many visits to the shoemaker after I'd been ice skating.

Some of the boys usually played a home-style game of hockey while we just skated around, trying to stay out of their way. Often the puck ended up on the surface ice of the creek and the other boys would dare the one who had hit it there to go get it. They also dared each other as well as the younger kids to skate on the creek. However, this was one promise I had made to my parents that I intended to keep. I never had the courage to test my luck on those frozen waters that were deeper and almost brooding at this time of year. Besides, almost every year, toward the end of winter when the ice was weak, at least one of the boys fell in. The water still wasn't deep enough for them to drown, but they got plenty wet and cold and had to walk home, sometimes as far as the top of the village, wearing their frozen clothes. Once they reached home they probably had their bottoms warmed up good by their fathers.

When we had our fill of sledding or ice skating, and if more fresh snow had fallen, we often built a snowman. We rolled the snow of the front lawn into three big balls, each one bigger than the last one, sometimes so big that Papa had to stack them on top of each other for us, using the smallest one for the head. Two small branches from under the trees served as arms, and we wound an old but colorful scarf that Mutti had loaned us around its neck. The coals we used for heating were perfect for eyes and for the mouth since they were pressed into oval shapes, kind of like eggs. If we didn't have a carrot, we used the coals for the nose as well. And Papa always loaned us one of his old hats to give our snowman a finished look. If we had a long stretch of cold days, we were able to greet our frozen friend every day for a long time. But we were always sad when the weather turned warm and we had to watch him melt away.

The snow forts and igloos we tried to build never worked out. The walls never stuck together or they collapsed shortly after we'd finished one, so we gave up on them. And I shied away from the snowball fights some of the kids had, after a small rock found its way into a snowball that hit me in the eye and made me see stars for a while. The area around the eye turned a beautiful shade of purple. The thing that upset me most, however, was when one of my teachers accused me of having been in a fight. That was something girls just didn't do and the teacher should have known that. I was so mortified just at the thought of this that I didn't realize that my instructor had been teasing me.

Ursula (Winter) Turner

Chapter 22
Christmas on Both Sides of the War

As far back as I can remember, we never missed celebrating one single Christmas, in spite of the war that was tearing up the country. I don't recall if we always had a Christmas tree, but I do know that we always had an Advent wreath to mark the holidays.

Although, during the war years and for some time afterward, there was never much by way of gifts, the Christmas holidays were always a special time for our small family.

Our Christmas season started with us observing Advent. Mutti always made our Advent wreath herself, using wire and live pine boughs she brought back from our trips to the woods. Four candles were placed evenly on the wreath with clip-on candle holders and she wound some red ribbon around the greenery. During the war she used whatever candles were on hand, but she told me she preferred fat, red candles, which she did use in later years. The wreath was then placed in the center of the small table in the living room.

Four Sundays before Christmas, after supper, and after the dishes had been washed and put away, Mutti, Mechthild and I, and later Papa as well, sat around the table and Mutti lit one of the candles while Mechthild turned off the lights. In the early days we said some prayers, especially for Papa's safe return before he came back to us. And we sang Christmas songs, and Mutti told Christmas tales, with the original Christmas story being told on the last Sunday before the big day. This was always a special time for me, making me feel protected and all warm inside, and I loved looking at the candles and

One of Mutti's Advent wreaths

their flickering flames, while listening to the stories. The following Sunday two candles were lit, and so on, until, on the last Sunday before Christmas all four candle flames shimmered and sparkled on the wreath, outdoing the 25-watt bulbs we were made to use in our light fixtures. The Advent wreath and the little ceremony that went with it was one of my favorite times of the Christmas season, but came in third after the number-one-rated *Bescherung* (the receiving of gifts) and St. Nikolaus day, which, in my estimation, rated number two.

    I always looked forward to St. Nikolaus day, which came along on December 6, the name day of St. Nikolaus. On this day most children in the neighborhood, in fact, in most of Germany, place their shoes on the floor outside of their door because they know, sometime during the course of the evening, Nikolaus will leave some small gift in them, such as a tiny doll or a sewing kit for girls, and small cars or tools for boys. During the war there was usually an apple and some cookies as well. After the war the apple was often replaced by a fat orange and candy might be added as well.

I normally didn't get to see Nikolaus on this day, although he did pay us a later visit. During the course of the evening, no matter how often I ran to the door, my shoes were always empty. He usually came when I was playing with my toys, and usually Mutti or Papa would tell me that they thought they had heard loud steps outside near the door and, perhaps, I should have another look to see if Nikolaus had been there this time and had left me something. Of course, by then he had and I had missed catching him at it again.

Sometimes a neighbor would be asked to dress up as St. Nikolaus and come to a house where a child needed special attention for having been naughty. If the misdeed had been small, a paddle might be left in one of the shoes as a reminder instead of Nikolaus making a special appearance.

I was "privileged" to become personally acquainted with St. Nikolaus just one time. I was still sucking my thumb, way beyond the time when children normally stop this habit, in spite of everything my parents had done to dissuade me from the nasty practice, such as putting pepper or some other unpleasant tasting spice on my thumb or placing a leather cover over it, something that was usually used to protect an injured finger. They tied the string in a knot around my wrist and I was unable to untie it with one hand, but I gnawed a hole into the tip of the thing until I could push it back and thereby free my thumb. They had also tried plain talking. Nothing had worked.

So, on one particular St. Nikolaus day Papa had asked a neighbor to play Nikolaus and told him what he wanted him to say to me. We were sitting around the living room table playing Parcheesi when the doorbell rang. When Papa volunteered to go to the door instead of sending one of us girls I knew something was up. My heart started to pound when I heard heavy footsteps come down the long hallway. Then I heard somebody talk to Papa in a deep voice. Could it be Nikolaus?

Suddenly, there he stood, right in front of me. He looked exactly like the one in my picture book except I couldn't see his smile because he was wearing a mean-looking mask. But he did have a big, white beard, wore a red, hooded, long robe and big black boots, and was carrying a burlap sack on his shoulder that looked heavy and had a switch sticking out of it.

"I heard you haven't been good last year," Nikolaus said in his deep voice. "Your Papa tells me that a big girl like you is still sucking her thumb. Aren't you ashamed of yourself? If you don't stop acting like a baby and keep sucking your thumb," he threatened, "there will be no gifts for you this Christmas." Then he reached for his sack which he had placed on the floor, threw it back over his shoulder, and turned toward the door. "Remember," he growled, "no gifts unless you stop sucking your thumb." Papa accompanied him back to the front door.

But even St. Nikolaus couldn't break me of my bad habit. I continued sucking my thumb for at least another couple of years, despite his threats and despite the warnings that my teeth would stick out like a rabbit's and that my thumb would end up flat, neither of which happened, by the way. Nor was I overlooked that Christmas at the *Bescherung*.

Our tree was never put up until Christmas Eve, which is the custom in a lot of German households, and most German families have their *Bescherung* in the evening of that day. It was Mutti's job to decorate the tree. She used real candles and had to be careful where she placed them on the tree, making sure there were no branches immediately above each candle. That was how Heidi and I knew how to place the candles on our tree in the basement. The tinsel she used was always saved from the previous year, especially during the war since none could be bought then, although she did add some when it was available again. The colorful balls were the same ones Mutti and Papa had bought for their first Christmas. When the tree twinkled and glittered in all its glory, Mutti placed everyone's gifts on small tables around the room, a special one for each person, but never under the tree. That was the place of honor for the nativity set.

One of our Christmas trees, featuring real candles

During the war years Mechthild and I had to stay in the kitchen which was kept warm on this evening, while Mutti got everything ready in the living room where a fire had also been lit. Lenchen Oma, who often visited us, kept us company in the kitchen if she was there, until we heard the silvery tinkle of a small bell, the signal that we were now allowed to come to the living room to see what the *Christkind* (Christ Child) had brought us.

I didn't know for a long time that it was Mutti who decorated the tree. I just assumed she wasn't with us in the kitchen because she was doing some kind of work in another part of the apartment.

After Papa returned, he always took us to the special evening services held at the old Lutheran Church located halfway up the hill, the only church in town. Mutti always stayed home from that service and I never questioned the reason for this. I suspect I didn't because of the excitement of the season. It wasn't until I was older that I learned what her role was in our Christmas Eve tradition.

The Lutheran Church in Allendorf

One year, during the war, I found what I thought was a brand-new doll among my gifts and I hugged my new baby and was very happy to add her to my doll family. Mutti told me later that the doll was an old one of Mechthild's that I had played with for a while, but was not able to recognize because of some changes. The doll had, at one time, boasted a full head of beautiful hair. I had brushed her curls so vigorously that it had left the dolly all but bald, so I'd stuck her in a corner of my play area and forgot about her.

Ursula (Winter) Turner

Mutti had not been able to find a new doll for me to take her place, so she decided to restore this one by giving her some new yarn hair and sewing and knitting her some different clothes. She painstakingly wove the yarn into the cloth-covered scalp until the doll had a full head of hair again. There was a problem, however. The only color of yarn Mutti had been able to lay her hands on was gray. Consequently, I gave my semi-new doll the name Oma because only Omas (grannies) had gray hair.

I could always count on receiving a few new items of clothing for Christmas that Mutti had worked on late into the night after Mechthild and I had gone to bed. Mechthild got new clothes, too, of course. Mine were often made from old ones of Mutti's that had been embellished with embroidery to make the items look pretty. All of our clothes were what Mutti called timeless, meaning they wouldn't go out of style like fad clothing did and could be worn until they didn't fit any more. This didn't bother me when I was little, but as I grew older I wanted to fit in with my friends, especially when I started to go to school in the city. I was considered a country hick by my classmates who all lived in the city. However, Mutti continued to make my timeless dresses with only the hem lengths changing according to the latest fashions. My frugal mother did this, of course, to save money since I could wear these clothes until I outgrew them or wore them out.

For the same reason I was only permitted three pairs of shoes at a time. One pair was for good (church, school, and other special occasions); one pair was for everyday (usually for playing outside); and the third pair was for sports (mostly gym which we had in middle school). The latter were made of canvas and rubber and laced up in the front. They were an ugly shade of brown which never changed from year to year. Whenever I needed new ones it seemed they could only be found in this one color. Because of the rubber they made my feet smell if I wore them too long. They were called tennis shoes, and all of my friends wore the same kind of shoes, although I don't remember any of the kids ever wearing them to play tennis since there were no tennis courts anywhere in our neighborhood. In addition I had my pair of boots for winter.

Even later, after the war, I can't remember ever receiving expensive gifts for Christmas. Besides the clothing, there might be a box of assorted chocolates and a book or a game. One year I remember finding a cheap wristwatch among my gifts. The only expensive gift I ever received was a bicycle which I needed after I finished fourth grade and went to school in Haiger. It was to be my summer transportation. I had learned to ride a bike using Mutti's old one, the one she took to go bartering for food. On the Christmas when I received my own bike, which they had been thoughtful enough to buy in my favorite color, green, I wanted to try it out right away and was very upset when Papa told me I could not ride it in the snow.

As I mentioned earlier, not much by way of diversions, such as movies or theater performances were available in Allendorf. But right before Christmas the school children of the little town were the ones to provide some entertainment during this particular time of year. Each grade practiced for weeks in preparation for the big day, when we all did our best to offer our school Christmas program by doing small skits, singing Christmas songs and reenacting the Christmas story for our relatives and friends and other townspeople. Mothers sewed costumes for angels and shepherds and all the other parts in the play, and fathers worked on the scenery, so everybody was involved in order to make the big holiday show a success.

Our school was too small to have an auditorium, and the classrooms certainly were not large enough to hold all the townspeople who would want to come and see the performances. So our Christmas show was always staged in the large backroom of one of the taverns, where occasionally a movie was shown and sometimes dances were held.

Most of the people of our small village were related to at least one of the children and came to give their support, but they also expected to be entertained by them.

This was a big day for us and it always ended with Nikolaus making a second appearance where we all got to see him, with his huge sack filled with goodies that had been donated by local businesses and had been bagged, with names attached, by volunteers, mostly consisting of mothers and teachers. Nikolaus usually sat in a chair and called our names, and we went up to him, sometimes hesitantly, to receive our bag of treats. The gifts were given to us in appreciation of our entertainment efforts and, of course, because it was Christmas. One year one of the gifts was a cutlery set made up of a fork, a spoon and a knife with the name Allendorf and the initials of the men's singing group that had donated it engraved on the handles. I don't know what happened to the spoon and knife, but I still have the fork.

* * *

During our Christmas visits to Launsbach, my family celebrated the holidays twice, the first part at Winter Oma's and Opa's house where the tree was set up in the parlor, a small room that was seldom used and never heated except on special occasions such as Christmas. A parlor was not really needed in a farmhouse since most visitors were simple folk who didn't have one of their own and preferred to visit in the kitchen. But since this house had an extra room, Oma decided to make it into a parlor, something she evidently used to have in her childhood home in southern Germany. By the time we gathered in this room for Christmas, it was still somewhat chilly because the fire had only been lit shortly before we had entered. Where my parents were frugal, my paternal grandparents were almost stingy, and they did not want to waste any wood or coal.

After opening our gifts, which must not have been very noteworthy because I can't remember one single item I received from Winter Oma and Opa for Christmas throughout the years, we had a light supper and lots of cookies. Then it was time for my parents, my sister and me to put on our warm, outdoor clothes in preparation for walking to Lenchen Oma's house to celebrate Christmas once again, this time with her, and with Tante Gertrud and the boys.

It seemed like we always had a white Christmas in those days. Since I was not normally allowed outside after dark, it was quite an experience for me to walk between my parents down the middle of the street through the crunchy snow. Sometimes I held lightly onto Mutti's and Papa's hands and looked up at the sky which was filled to overflowing with coldly glittering stars. When Mechthild was there, she usually trailed behind us.

At Lenchen Oma's house the boys had been waiting impatiently for us to make our appearance because they had not been allowed to unwrap their gifts until we arrived. I don't remember any of the gifts I received here either, but I always had fun at my cousins' house because I got to play with their toy cars. Papa didn't believe girls should receive cars for gifts which meant I had to settle for dolls and related items. But he did let me play with Jürgen's and Gunter's cars since that was just for a short time.

*   *   *

Prior to Christmas Eve, not many holiday decorations could be found in most homes. In ours there was the Advent wreath with its greenery and candles, and there was my Advent calendar that hung on the wall, waiting to have one of its 23 windows opened by my eager hands, one each day of December until, on December 24, when I was finally able to open the big door. And there might be a few decorations I had made in school. Therefore, on Christmas Eve, the tree with its flickering candles and glittering icicles and colorful ornaments appeared awesome to me and, although my memory is vague on most of the gifts I received, the scent of real pine at Christmas time will always place me back to the Christmas celebrations of my youth.

Sirens

Epilogue
Leaving Allendorf

In Germany teachers are hired, and also transferred, at the discretion of the state, the same way servicemen are transferred in the United States. However, if a teacher has been on the job for a long time and asks to be transferred to a certain place, the request is usually granted. This was the case with Papa.

For some time he and Mutti had wanted to move back to their hometown. Launsbach was the village where both of my parents had been born and where they grew up, and they wanted very much to move back there to be with family and friends. However the stumbling block that prevented this move was that there was only one school in Launsbach, and the position of principal was already filled.

Although Winter Oma was the only one of my grandparents still alive by then, Mutti's sister, Tante Gertrud, and Papa's sister, whom we all called Got, still lived there. Papa's youngest brother, Onkel Emil, lived in the next town over the hill, just a short walking distance away for Papa, who never did learn to drive a car. Besides the bicycle, which was his general mode of transportation and for which the hill was too steep, Papa had only ever driven a motorcycle, and that was many years ago when he was a very young man.

Then fate lent a hand in granting my parents their wish. A brand-new school was being built in Launsbach, but, sadly, before the school's principal was able to start his first school year there, he died of a heart attack. Papa's sister informed him of this, knowing he would want to apply for the position. She had to do it by mail since we didn't have a phone, so it took a little while for the news to reach him, but he immediately applied for the job, as did several other principals as well as some well qualified teachers.

Mutti longed to go back home where she still knew a number of people with whom she had kept in touch during our numerous vacation visits. She and Papa were nervous wrecks during the next several weeks. They worried that Papa's war record might be held against him, even though he had been cleared of any wrongdoing, as well as of having been a true Nazi. They thought that the people who were in charge of hiring wouldn't know Papa for the upstanding man he was. They also worried that one of the other applicants might be better qualified than Papa. It seemed like an eternity to them before the notification arrived. I wasn't sure what outcome I was hoping for. I hated to leave my hometown and with that all my friends. I also dreaded the thought of attending a new school. But I liked Launsbach where my grandmother and my aunts, but most of all, where my cousins lived. And my parents assured me that I could always make new friends. At any rate, Papa got the job, and he got it for two reasons. First, the citizens of Allendorf respected him and, although they hated to lose him, they had given him an excellent rating, both as teacher and as principal and, secondly, Launsbach was his and Mutti's hometown and people there knew him as a hard worker and said so when asked.

Mechthild was no longer living with us by then. She had married and was making her home in Wetzlar, the same town we had to travel through to get to Launsbach and where we always had to wait so long for our train connections. The last big celebration in our school apartment had been her wedding. Mechthild had decided to marry in the place where we had lived for so long and where so many noteworthy events had taken place. She and her new husband Heinz, one of the refugees from Eastern Europe, came one last time to assist us with the packing.

Sirens

I tearfully said good-bye to my classmates in Haiger. I was leaving a school of about 400 students, both boys and girls, to attend a school of 2,000 students – all girls. The only males around were teachers. Ricarda Huch Schule was located in Gießen, 5 kilometers (a little more than 3 miles) from Launsbach. I had to take the regular bus to get there and then walk several blocks along city streets that were still lined with the rubble of houses that had been destroyed by bombs, to reach the school, which had also lost one wing during an air-raid.

In Launsbach we, once again, lived upstairs in what was the old school. People were no longer following the old custom of having the teachers live in the school building, and the new school was not outfitted with any apartments. But we only lived in the old school until the construction of our own house was completed. The former classrooms of the old building were being utilized by the mayor and the town's government. Ours was the only apartment in the building which was smaller than the one in Allendorf.

It took a couple more years before we were able to move into our own home where the second floor had been finished first so Mechthild and Heinz could live there. Heinz rode the train to Wetzlar to his job and later changed to a job closer to home. Mechthild no longer worked outside the home but became a housewife.

The interior walls of our house were constructed entirely of bricks from bombed houses. They cost less but created a lot of work for us since we had to sit around the building site of our house for days using hammers to knock off the old mortar to make the bricks usable. My hands soon were worn raw by the rough mortar and bricks.

Ursula (Winter) Turner

Mutti is knocking mortar off bricks from bombed houses. The bricks were used to build our own house. They were cheaper than new bricks

Sirens

When we finally moved into the house, my room was upstairs, part of my sister's apartment, and I had a wonderful view of a section of the village, some fields, the Lahn River and, in the distance, the city of Gießen.

I visited Allendorf a couple of times, but transportation continued to be complicated between my former and new home. When I took the train, I still had that long wait in the station at Wetzlar. And the one time I talked a girlfriend into taking our bikes there, we got a ticket for riding along the highway without using our hands.

In 1960, one year after marrying an American soldier, the two of us took our baby son to start a new life in America. I had heard so much about this country and, after meeting those first G.I.s as a child, I knew I would like living here – and I do!

Ursula (Winter) Turner

Author's Note

Today I live in a small town in peaceful Kansas, where I am, however, again haunted by sirens.

Each spring, during the tornado season, when one of these monsters comes particularly close to us, the terrifying wailing of the siren pierces the air of the darkened, rain-lashed town to warn us that one of these dangerous storms is in the vicinity and might be heading our way. But while my husband and the neighbors seek shelter in basements or cellars and are contemplating the destruction a tornado is capable of causing, I am taken back to the sound of the sirens and to the basement and cellar shelters of my youth. And the hair at the nape of my neck stands up while goose bumps form on my skin, and for an instant I seem to hear the droning sound of approaching airplane engines. And for just one short moment I am back, living through the horrifying events of World War II.

Sirens

Other works by Ursula (Winter) Turner

A Mother's Sins

Hello There… Have a Nice Day

For Information:
Ursula Turner
uturnj@sbcglobal.net